AFTERGLOW

TROY KOTANIDES

Copyright ©2025 Troy Kotanides

ISBN: 978-1-957917-84-9 (paperback)
ISBN: 978-1-957917-85-6 (e-book)

Library of Congress Control Number: 2025915594

All rights reserved. No part of this book may be reproduced, stored in a retrieval system, or transmitted in any form or by any means without prior written permission from the author, except for the use of brief quotations in a book review.

Cover design by Judith S. Design & Creativity
www.judithsdesign.com
Published by Glass Spider Publishing
www.glassspiderpublishing.com

Keep me in your memories, Edyn
This is our goodbye
But I know I won't lose you forever, because
You'll still be where you've always been

1
SUPPRESSION

"It's been a couple of years since you've been to see me, Edyn. I'm so glad you decided to come back." The man extended his hand. "Doctor Gordon Raine. You do remember me, don't you?"

Edyn shook the doctor's hand. "Of course I do, Doctor—"

"Please, just call me Raine," the doctor quickly interjected before guiding Edyn to his chair. "You remember that's what I go by here."

Edyn took a deep breath and hesitantly sat in the chaise lounge chair nearby. This was the first time in two years he had been back to see his psychologist, and he was incredibly nervous. He had never been comfortable opening up about his issues and emotions to someone else, which was why he'd stopped seeing Raine years ago in the first place, but he knew he needed to try *something*. Especially with what was happening to him lately.

The room hadn't changed much since the last time Edyn had been there. It was small and comforting, with Raine's mahogany desk as the centerpiece, matching the surrounding wood-textured walls, and a small bookshelf to its right. The office had a colorful and lively look as Raine always made sure to have a few plants growing, one of which being the large fern next to Edyn's chair.

AFTERGLOW

Natural sunlight flooded the room through large windows that covered the upper half of the left wall facing Edyn. It didn't have the feeling of a doctor's office, and Edyn liked that.

Raine took the chair to Edyn's right, as he often did with his patients. Sitting beside them, rather than behind his desk, made their sessions feel more personal and less intimidating.

Now toward the twilight stages of his career, Raine captured the appearance of someone from another era. He was a traditionalist in every sense of the word—never deviating too far from his usual collared shirt paired with dress slacks, with the occasional sweater vest overtop when he was feeling adventurous. He appeared just the same as Edyn had remembered: slender with a calm, clean-shaven face, and hair that was almost purely white, matching the slim white dress shirt he wore.

As Edyn studied him further, the doctor proceeded to skim through his notes. "You know, I had just determined my diagnosis for you the last we met, but you stopped coming in before we could progress any further." He hesitated a moment, then slowly looked up at Edyn. "I will admit, this is one of my most difficult diagnoses, and your case is an unusual one at that. I can assure you, though, with proper therapy, cases even as drastic as yours can fully resolve themselves."

Edyn felt uneasy about the positivity Raine was displaying as he thought back on his first session with the doctor nearly two years ago.

"So you can't remember anything at all prior to a year ago, is that correct?" Raine had asked him, a hint of skepticism in his voice.

Edyn responded with only a subtle nod of his head, acknowledging his strange situation.

1: SUPPRESSION

It was true—Edyn had no retained memories prior to a year ago, and his earliest memories from that point in time were clouded.

The first memory he could recall was taking refuge in a warehouse at the nearby docks. The dock workers had claimed they found Edyn lying on the shore, wet and disoriented, and in a state of confusion. Edyn could barely utter words, let alone offer an explanation as to why he was there. When the workers weren't getting any kind of response about where he'd come from, they brought in their manager to deal with him.

Eventually, Edyn gained the strength to speak and the dock manager sensed sincerity in his claims about not knowing where he was and having no home or possessions. Viewing him as harmless, he decided to give Edyn time to recuperate and allowed him to stay in the warehouse temporarily, using the break area for rest. This was all in exchange for cheap labor, of course.

In the weeks that followed, the dock manager used his vast local connections to help Edyn as much as the situation allowed. Eventually, he offered Edyn an official job at the warehouse, helped him relocate to a low-cost furnished apartment nearby, and assisted him in obtaining necessary "legitimate" documentation.

Raine's curious voice interrupted Edyn's reminiscing. "You don't have any family, and nobody has tried to contact you?"

Edyn shook his head and responded in a deflated tone. "No. I don't have any family that I know of, and it doesn't seem anyone is looking for me. I truthfully can't remember anything before a year ago. I have no recollection at all."

"Quite peculiar indeed..." Raine's eyes wandered, a puzzled look on his face as he scratched at his chin. "Certainly, there must be something from your past that you remember. A feeling, an image, or maybe something from your childhood?"

Edyn felt frustrated with the doctor, who sounded as if he didn't believe him.

But there *was* one thing Edyn could remember. At least he thought he could. He wasn't sure if it truly was a memory. He looked at Raine, his gaze firm, and responded with only two words: "A hill."

I'll try to stick around this time.

Edyn returned his focus to the present, and on Raine, while the doctor read through his notes. "Ah, yes. Psychogenic amnesia. That's what I believe you are experiencing, and that was my previous diagnosis." He glanced up at Edyn and continued with an assured tone. "I've dealt with cases like yours for almost thirty-five years, Edyn. Stay positive, stay with me, and I am certain we will solve this."

He turned to the next page of his notes and continued. "I want to discuss in further detail the nature of this condition so you can understand it, accept it, and be able to overcome it."

Raine turned to set his notes on the desk, then glanced gently at Edyn. "First, though, let's talk about how you're doing. You left so abruptly last time that I had hoped your condition had cleared up, and that's why you never returned." He adjusted his glasses, and with a more concerned look on his face, added, "Now tell me—what made you come back?"

Feeling uneasy, Edyn shifted in his chair, stalling for time.

How can I explain this?

He knew what he needed to tell Raine, but finding the right words was difficult, especially since Edyn didn't fully understand what was happening himself. Finally, he mustered up a hesitant response. "I've been having… weird thoughts lately." He paused, searching for the right words. "Well, maybe not thoughts, but

1: SUPPRESSION

more like visions. I don't know…"

Edyn cast a glance at the floor and continued. "These visions—they've always happened on occasion, but they're happening a lot more often now. And I've been getting these headaches, too." He took a deep breath and added, "I… I just took a temporary leave from work because of all this, hoping my head would clear up."

To Edyn's shock, Raine responded excitedly, "I am glad to hear that!"

Huh?

"Taking time off from work and giving your brain a break is always beneficial in dealing with issues of the mind," Raine expanded. "It amazes me how little we understand about how much daily stresses affect our minds and worsen our symptoms. Giving your mind a 'vacation' is always something I suggest to my patients."

I wouldn't call being here a vacation.

The gears in Raine's head seemed to be churning at full speed. "Now, about this vision that you are having. Would it happen to be of the hill you mentioned previously? That was one of the last notes I had jotted down years ago."

"Yes," Edyn replied. "It's the same vision I've always had. I really don't know if it's a memory or not, but I'm remembering more of it now. And it feels so *real*."

Raine seemed to grow suddenly more hopeful. "Yes, yes. I believe this may be a memory from some time in the past that's trying to come back out. Can you expand upon this hill? Can you describe its form? Can you tell me exactly what it is you're seeing when you think of it?"

Edyn shook his head. "That's the thing. I'm not exactly thinking about it, and I'm not trying to remember anything. The memory, or whatever it is, comes out of nowhere when it happens, and it feels like I'm actually there."

Raine seemed puzzled as Edyn proceeded to describe the vision in further detail.

"It's been happening for a while—as long as I can remember. Always the same image when it happens: I'm sitting at the top of a small grassy hill at night overlooking the sea, with water crashing into the rocks below. Above, a gigantic version of the moon is hanging in the sky. It's maybe ten times larger than it usually appears."

Edyn hesitated before revealing the final part to Raine. His voice quivered when he spoke. "I feel a terrible sadness when I experience it. When it happens, someone—a woman—is speaking to me."

Raine was feverishly jotting down notes as Edyn finished describing the scene. Strangely, Edyn noticed a look of confidence on Raine's face as he wrote, his head nodding the entire time. It was as if Raine was hearing something he'd been expecting. Maybe even something he'd been hoping for.

Finally, Raine set his pen down. "Ah, yes. I believe this memory may be a key to helping your condition, as well as opening your mind further. I know you don't quite understand if it's a memory or not, but you clearly feel close to it emotionally. From your description, it doesn't sound like any place around here that I am aware of. It's possible it could be a memory that has become clouded, or *changed*, but with the core of the memory remaining intact. But let's not jump to any conclusions just yet."

Raine stood and walked to his desk. He set down his notes, picked up a stack of printed papers, and brought them back over with him. "This is a great starting point for us, Edyn, and we will come back to this vision. But first, I think it's important for you to better understand the nature of your condition." He sat back down

1: SUPPRESSION

in his chair. "It's a beautiful way in which they work. Our minds, that is. A condition such as yours gets interpreted negatively, but once you can see the beauty in it, it can become much easier to understand, accept, and resolve."

Edyn began to feel better about his decision to come back and see Dr. Raine. "Psychogenic amnesia," Edyn said to the doctor. "That's what you called it, right?"

Raine nodded confidently. "Yes. Based on the description of your condition, I am certain that this is what you're experiencing. The addition of a powerful, recurring memory that you are close to emotionally provides even more evidence."

Edyn squirmed in his chair at Raine's confirmation. "But that doesn't sound good, though, right?"

I mean, it has "psycho" in the word.

"Don't be troubled," Raine said reassuringly. "It has nothing to do with being 'good' or not. It is just a very specific and very rare type of amnesia. As I mentioned before, I personally think it's a beautiful thing, and I want you to see it that way too."

Edyn gave a cautious nod and found a little more courage. "What can you tell me about it?"

"Psychogenic amnesia is in the category we refer to as 'retrograde amnesia.' In cases such as this, the brain loses its ability to retrieve stored memories up to the point of the onset of the amnesia. However, the ability to form new memories is retained."

The doctor paused briefly before continuing. "This condition is usually induced by physiological triggers rather than by a physical cause. In minor cases, the brain may be unable to retrieve only certain, specific memories due to stress or a minor trauma. In more serious cases, however, the brain suppresses *all* memories due to an incredibly severe trauma, preventing the patient from remembering anything leading up to and including the traumatic event itself."

Raine looked intently into Edyn's eyes, his concern over the severity of Edyn's condition showing through them. "Your case is leaning more toward the latter." He skimmed through a few pages of the printout on his lap. "But you'll be happy to know that based on your previous lab results and scans that we have on file, there was no discovered physical damage to your hippocampus or any other parts of your brain. You don't have any discernible brain damage. This is purely mental, Edyn."

A confused look crossed Edyn's face. "Why should that make me feel better about my condition?"

Raine sat up straight in his chair, and his eyes widened. "Because, Edyn, that means there isn't anything with your condition that can't be fixed. You don't have irreversible brain damage. With proper therapy, we can unlock what is being concealed by your mind, and this condition can clear itself." Then, with a sense of emphasis, he added, "You know, the word 'trauma' itself shouldn't worry you all that much anyway. The word derives from the Greek word for 'wound.' And what do we know about wounds?" The doctor paused to let his rhetorical question set in before concluding, "That they can heal. That they *will* heal."

Edyn felt a glimmer of hope. For the first time, he was truly reassured that what was happening to him could be helped—and possibly, cured.

But deep down, he felt that his situation was different from others. He hadn't told Raine everything yet.

"Your case, unfortunately, is severe. It troubles me that you can't remember anything from your past prior to three years ago, nor your own personal information. Although it's common in these types of cases for the patient to be unable to remember who they are, and to lose these 'declarative memories' as we refer to

1: SUPPRESSION

them, it does suggest that a major trauma took place which caused the onset of the amnesia."

Raine took a deep breath before continuing his explanation of the frightening nature of this condition.

"The memory of the trauma is being unconsciously suppressed by the brain so that you cannot experience the pain associated with it any further. Your brain is trying to protect you. Because of this, unfortunately, it comes at the expense of all your other memories leading up to that point as well. Shutters have been cast over them, blocking the rays of their reach."

Although Edyn listened closely, there was still a large part of him that remained skeptical.

"I just find this hard to believe, Doctor," Edyn interjected. "My brain just completely 'shut off' because of some trauma and, just like that, all my memories vanished? There had to be something else other than just a traumatic event that caused this. There had to be some sort of injury or *something*, right?"

...*Right?*

Raine stood and paced a few steps, as if to buy some time before responding to his distraught patient. "I can see why you are confused and can't quite understand. But I can assure you that your brain most certainly did not 'shut off,' as you put it. Quite the contrary. We can re-run the imaging of your brain if that would make you feel more comfortable, but the previous results were conclusive: There wasn't any physical damage." Raine paused for a moment and glanced upward, softly thinking aloud. "Hmm... how can I describe this better?"

He began to pace around the room in thought. He realized he had described the end result of Edyn's condition—the "what"—but understood how this could worry his patient and cause him to see only the negative aspects of it. He realized he needed to help

Edyn understand the "why" and view the reason behind it in a more positive light.

After formulating some ideas, Raine turned back to Edyn, describing the condition to him in a different way. "You know, there are some theories claiming that this condition is a type of 'self-preservation' by the body, as it's protecting itself and its brain from experiencing any further pain. It's not necessarily that your brain has 'shut off' in any way. Actually, one could argue that just the opposite has occurred, and certain hidden abilities within the brain have been unlocked, or activated!"

Raine walked back toward Edyn, eager to continue his explanation. "There is so much we don't understand about the inner workings of our minds. There are capabilities within that simply cannot be measured or understood, and probably never will. Therein lies the beauty of the way with which the mind works and the abilities it has." The doctor gazed into Edyn's eyes with sincere care. "It's possible that your brain's abilities just came into action more readily than others' would have. It's a defense mechanism." Raine sat back down next to Edyn. "You might even say your brain is working at a higher capacity than others, and that is what caused all of this to happen. It is a truly clever condition, and it takes a truly clever mind. Incredibly, the brain can wipe out all memory recollection yet still retain the necessary learned skills and 'procedural memories' that allow you to function in daily life. Thought processes, motor skills, math, information learned—all retained as if nothing ever happened, while your memories remain suppressed. What a mysteriously beautiful thing the mind is, and yours appears to be at the higher end of this beauty. Do you see now what I am trying to get you to understand?"

Edyn took a moment to process Raine's words. He found comfort in the message and it began to help him see his condition

1: SUPPRESSION

in a new light.

Maybe he's right?

"I do see. I just didn't know that any of this was even possible, and I figured there had to be something physical to blame."

Raine smiled and gave a slight chuckle. "It's a good thing you didn't know everything already. I would be out of a job if you did!"

Raine stood and walked over to the water cooler nestled tightly in the corner near the closed door. "Would you like some water?"

"Sure," Edyn replied, feeling as if he didn't have much of a choice since Raine had already grabbed two paper cups.

The doctor filled them and handed one to Edyn. He sipped slowly. "I'd like to keep having these sessions with you, Dr. Raine," he said. "I hope we can schedule more soon while I'm off work, if that's alright with you."

"Heavens, yes!" Raine immediately answered. "We can have as many as you'd like. I'd like to get you back in tomorrow, actually, for a longer session. Afterward, I will review my schedule and try to get you in every couple of days while you are on leave. And of course, once that period has ended, we can determine a more structured schedule of regular sessions going forward."

Edyn liked Dr. Raine's game plan but wanted to talk to him about something else that was troubling him while there was still time in today's session. "That sounds good to me, Doctor. But there's something else I've been experiencing that I was hoping to talk to you about today—"

Raine quickly interjected, "Enough with this 'Doctor' nonsense. I'm going to be your friend throughout this, Edyn, so just call me Raine. And as far as anything else you've been experiencing, let's save that for tomorrow's session when we have more time together. I don't want us to get too scattered just yet." Raine continued, his tone more purposeful. "I would like us to first focus more on this recurring vision that you described. With the recent uptick in occurrences, this suggests that you may have already begun making progress on your own, as your mind appears to be wanting you to remember. With help, I believe we can speed up this process even more."

Raine stopped for a moment, seemingly lost in thought, his eyes drifting away. "It's odd, though, now that I am thinking about it. Your first memories don't appear to be right after the memory of the hill, as is usually the case when dealing with the trauma of this condition. I know it was a clouded time for you, so it will be difficult to be sure, but there's also the possibility that your mind may have suppressed memories even for a time *after* the suspected trauma." Raine snapped back into focus. "Ah, but I digress. We don't even know yet if this is what triggered the event. We'll dive deeper into this tomorrow."

Edyn got out of his seat, sensing their time was ending. "I'm really glad I decided to come in today and... thank you, Raine, for believing me."

Raine smiled. "Of course, Edyn. I'm glad you decided to come back." He glanced down at the papers in his hands. "Before you leave, though—I'm looking over the information we have on file for you, and it's sparking my curiosity, if you have just another moment."

"Sure."

"So you can't remember anything from your childhood, but you can confirm your age as thirty-two, correct?" Raine asked.

"Yes," Edyn answered. "Well, at least, I think so. That's what it is according to my driver's license. My manager helped me with all that stuff a few years ago. Age, basic personal info, and so on." Edyn grew distraught thinking about these things. "It's weird, you know? It's almost like my birth date is irrelevant. Since I can't

1: SUPPRESSION

remember anything before three years ago, it feels like I was basically 'born' in 1991."

Raine gave a quirky laugh. "Then it shall be my job to age you!" Edyn flashed a quick smile for the first time today, and the doctor continued in a more serious tone. "I can understand, though, how that must make you feel, as it feels like your life has only just begun. But if you think about it, we have all gone through the same thing. It's no different from how children can't remember their infancy. No one can truly determine exactly when their first memories began. It is more than clouded for all of us, and it seems like we just 'appeared' one day and have been existing, and remembering, ever since."

Edyn had never thought of it that way before, and he wasn't sure whether it was supposed to make him feel better or not, but it did spark his thoughts. He also began to realize that goodbyes with Raine apparently took a while.

I think he's "digressing" again…

Cleverly, Edyn extended his hand for a shake to initiate his exit. Raine shook his hand tightly, but didn't let him leave just yet. "One more thing before you go, just out of curiosity." He paused, allowing a build-up to his final question. "As there isn't anything from your past that you can remember—can you tell me, if you don't mind, how you know your name is Edyn?"

It appeared the gears in Raine's head were still churning during this prolonged exit. The question caught Edyn completely off-guard and made him feel something terrible in the pit of his stomach. As opposed to his other personal information, which had been either fabricated or estimated, Edyn knew his own name for a distinctly different reason. He had always been reminded of it, for as long as he could remember. And as soon as Raine had asked the question, deep within the corridors of Edyn's shattered mind, the haunting answer came echoing from within.

Edyn looked directly into the doctor's eyes, and just before walking out the door, replied, "Because that's what she calls me."

2
SEASIDE

Edyn stepped out of the building that housed Raine's office, closed the door behind him, and inhaled a deep breath of the coastal summer breeze.

He was in the middle of the small uptown area of Riverwood Cove. The sounds of crying seagulls and gently crashing waves filled the air. Local shops and offices lined the east side of the street, with breathtaking views of densely forested inclining hills filling the background. On the opposite side, a small pier and boardwalk touched the sea. It was a calm and peaceful place—quite a forgotten small gem of the Pacific Northwest—but everyone here liked it that way.

He frequently traveled through this area on his way to work, as the docks were down the road about a mile north, but he rarely stopped by on his way to enjoy the setting. He knew he would have ample opportunity now that he'd be making regular visits.

Earlier, he'd made the short walk from his apartment to his appointment as he was worried about driving, given the troubles in his head lately.

It was now early evening, as Edyn was Raine's last appointment. Countless people mingled about the area, making their final visits to the local shops before closing time. Edyn watched them as he thought about the conversation he'd just had with Raine, still troubled by some lingering thoughts.

I didn't tell him everything.

That voice…

Edyn shook it off and headed down the lively street. People were making their way in and out of shops while others enjoyed the casual drive along the coast. Edyn took notice of the happiness on everyone's faces. He wondered if any of them also had things they were hiding.

He walked past a tavern and saw a large colorful poster on the front window. The design was scattered with illustrated guitars.

Live show this Friday!
Music starts at 6:00 p.m. sharp
as three local bands battle it out.
Don't be late!
Or be late. Whatever. Your call.
We'll still let you give us your money.

Edyn smiled to himself as he passed by. Just ahead, a family of four crossed the street with fishing rods in hand. They were heading the same direction as Edyn, likely hoping to get some evening catches in off the boardwalk.

He made his way to the end of the block and crossed the street to reach the boardwalk. He looked up as a group of seagulls flew past, silhouetted against the sun, its heat pressing against Edyn's face.

Is it really possible my mind has been hiding my memories from me?

Edyn was still skeptical about Raine's diagnosis, but knew he had to trust the doctor's judgment.

2: SEASIDE

As he lowered his gaze, he noticed numerous fliers pinned to the lamp posts scattered along the boardwalk.

Coastal Drilling Co. Grand Reopening
NOW HIRING – ALL POSITIONS

He marveled at the gentle waves rolling in as he walked down the boardwalk, but the serene moment proved short-lived.

After only a few short steps, Edyn felt a sharp pain in his head and began to feel dizzy. He tried to shake it off, but it rapidly intensified.

His vision swirled, and for brief moments the sea and boardwalk transformed into an ominous vision of a winding path up a grassy hill with a large moon hanging above.

It flashed before him in endless succession, each time accompanied by the sound of electrical waves and cracks. Fear and confusion gripped him, and the pain in his head worsened.

What is happening?!

The visions then morphed together, and Edyn could take no more, falling hard to the ground.

Staring straight down with his hands on his knees, he gathered himself. But when he peered up, he found himself atop the moonlit hill.

The sea crashed hard into the rocks below, and a terrible sadness came over Edyn as he experienced a familiar scene.

I know you'll be able to find me

Keep me in your memories, Edyn
This is our goodbye
But I know I won't lose you forever, because
You'll still be where you've always been

"Hey! Are you okay?"

He looked up to see a young boy with a fishing rod in hand standing above him. It was the same kid he'd seen moments earlier with his family. "Yeah," Edyn said as his mind began to clear. "I think so."

"Well, what are you doin' kneeling on the ground like that? I was gonna go get my mom 'cause I saw you fall, and then your eyes looked all weird."

Edyn looked past the kid to see the rest of his family nearby getting their fishing equipment set up. "I'll be okay, kid. Go ahead back to your parents."

The kid scurried off without another word, seemingly frightened by what he'd just seen.

Edyn climbed to his feet, though he still felt shaken. The vision was much more intense than usual.

As always, he couldn't see the woman speaking to him, he could only hear her voice echoing in his head. But he heard the woman speak just a few more words this time: *"I know you'll be able to find me."*

Who is she?

Edyn felt the need to get back home quickly to rest. He headed

2: SEASIDE

back across the street and began the trek back to his apartment, just past the cemetery outside of town.

He walked briskly past all the shops and offices from where he'd come until he reached the outskirts of the uptown Riverwood Cove area.

Here, he made his way through a residential area with beautifully landscaped houses on his left and stunning seaside houses on the right.

Ahead, the cemetery came into view, but as he drew near, the pain in his head returned. He picked up the pace, wanting to get home as quickly as possible before something else might happen, and soon reached the cemetery's open entrance gates.

He decided to cut through the cemetery instead of taking the longer route around it. He darted through the hilly graveyard, seeking openings between headstones and mausoleums to stay on a direct path. The statues of angels seemed to watch his every step.

He had just reached the center of the cemetery, gravestones all around, when the pain in his head intensified terribly, bringing him to a complete stop.

He braced his head with his right hand. His vision clouded and he grew dizzy. The headstones danced around him in a swirl, and he fell to his knees, struck by the same flashes and electrical sounds as before.

> We're going to be apart for a long time, but
> If you get lost
> Come back here
> Just like we promised
> I know you'll be able to find me

> Keep me in your memories, Edyn
> This is our goodbye
> But I know I won't lose you forever, because
> You'll still be where you've always been

The vision ended, followed by a powerful flash of light accompanied by more piercing electrical sounds. Through the noise, Edyn heard the haunting echo of a distinctly different voice speaking to him.

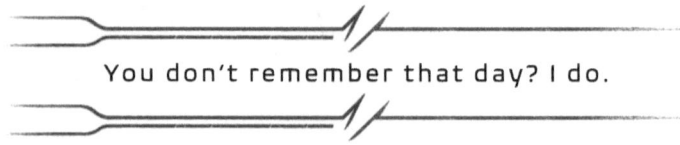

You don't remember that day? I do.

Edyn snapped back to his senses. An intense fear crawled inside of him.

Who was that?!

There was something undeniably powerful about the voice that echoed all around. It felt as if it was coming from everywhere at once, engulfing him. Shivers ran down Edyn's spine at the sound, but strangely, it was a familiar fear.

Edyn sat on his knees in the grass as he tried to shake off the fear, while crickets chirped loudly around him. He scanned the area, surprised to find himself in darkness. The sun had long set, and a thickening fog was creeping over the cemetery grounds.

How much time has passed?

Edyn stood and made his way as quickly as possible to the cemetery's exit. When he finally reached it, he traversed the incline of the street leading into the more forested part of town. He passed

2: SEASIDE

beneath pine trees that towered overhead as streetlights illuminated the way forward.

Soon, his apartment complex came into view. As he neared the building, he saw a woman walking from the parking lot at the back toward the main entrance where he was headed. Edyn recognized the woman's face. His heart skipped a beat.

The woman had wavy brown hair and wore a slim white sundress. When she saw Edyn, she stopped at the door, her amber eyes giving him a soft gaze. She smiled, and a nervousness came over him.

Why do I still get like this?

He returned her smile as he approached, reflecting on the time he met her five months ago.

What was that noise?

Edyn woke with a start at the sound of a loud thump coming from just outside his apartment door. He quickly threw on some clothes and rushed to the door to discover the source of the sound. He opened it and saw a woman across the hall struggling to pick up a large box.

"Can I give you a hand?" Edyn offered.

The woman gave Edyn a casual smile and let out a light laugh. "I thought I could get everything in myself, and hey, I almost made it."

The box lay on the ground, partially torn, with a few photos and picture frames spilling out. The woman extended her hand. "The name's Serah. Pleased to meet you, sir! Today's my moving-in day."

Edyn felt a natural excitement and smiled as he shook her hand, not realizing he was just staring at her.

"Well...?" she said. "You're supposed to tell me your name now, right?"

"Oh, sorry." Edyn gave a short, anxious laugh and finally released her hand. "My name's Edyn."

Pull it together, Edyn.

Serah gave him a somewhat surprised look. "Edyn, huh? That's a weird name. But I like it." She studied him a moment. "It doesn't sound like you're from around here, but you definitely look like you are."

Edyn noticed how quick-witted and clever Serah was. She seemed the type to say what was on her mind without hesitation. He knew what she meant, though. With his long brown hair down to his shoulders and plain clothes, Edyn resembled a lot of people living in the region. Although he didn't care much for it, he was familiar with the "grunge" term being thrown around lately.

Serah cut back in and made a notion to the box on the ground. "Well… are you just going to stand there?"

Edyn looked down and quickly realized his error. "Oh, sorry!"

Serah realized not all of her playful quips were getting through Edyn's more serious demeanor and decided to pick him back up a bit. "I dropped this one as I was trying to get it through the door. Saved the heaviest for last, of course." She gave a playful smile. "You look like you're a pretty strong guy, though. You should be able to handle it."

Edyn smiled nervously as he bent over to pick up the box. He noticed the old photos that had spilled out nearby and started to gather those first. Some of the photos showed a couple, but most were just of a single woman.

He set the photos on top of the heavier items in the box, then put his hands firmly underneath and lifted carefully.

As he stood up, Serah's face came back into view, and he saw that she was looking at him with a touch of sadness. "Those are my parents," she said, hesitating before continuing. "I don't see

2: SEASIDE

them anymore."

Before Edyn could muster up a response, Serah made a gesture and stepped into the doorway of her apartment.

"Here," she said, "follow me."

She guided him inside to a corner of her living room, where he set the box down next to many others just like it.

"Pretty convenient for you to only offer help once I'm on the *last* box," Serah playfully said, giving him a sarcastic look. Edyn laughed. "Nonetheless," she continued, "it was a noble gesture by you, my friend." She glanced around. "As you can see, my place is a mess right now, and I really don't feel like unpacking everything just yet. Also, I suppose I owe you something. So how about we head down the street to a café I saw on the way in, and I'll buy us a late Saturday morning coffee. Sound like a plan?"

Surprised, Edyn nodded nervously. "Sure, that sounds great."

Serah grabbed her purse off the kitchen counter and smirked to herself. Without looking at Edyn, she said, "You know, you might want to put on some *real* clothes first before we go."

Realizing he was still in his sweatpants and loose-fitting T-shirt, he let out another nervous laugh and promptly went back to his apartment to change.

Minutes later, the two were walking down the sidewalk side by side. Edyn smiled to himself, happy for the first time in a long while. Out of nowhere, he had made a new friend—and he didn't have many of those.

Edyn focused back on the present and approached his friend.

"What are you doing roaming the streets at this hour?" Serah asked him.

"What time *is* it?" Edyn asked in response.

Serah checked her watch and let out an audible sigh. "Almost

9:30. I'm just getting back from work, actually. There was a lot for us curatorial assistants to tear down tonight after closing, since it was the last day of our summer exhibits."

"Sorry to hear that," Edyn replied. "That's a long day of work."

Serah shrugged. "It is. But I gotta put in my time, and at least I'm off tomorrow. Off on a Friday. Can you believe it?"

"Wow, that's really nice."

"I know! I'm so excited for this weekend! It's going to be amazing! Off all day tomorrow for starters, then the season-two premiere of *The X-Files* is tomorrow night, and then our end-of-summer work party is Saturday evening at the museum hall after we close. Food, drinks, dancing, and beautiful late-summer weather are all in the forecast for the party!" She tried to contain her outward excitement by asking, in a more serious tone, "You still wanted to go to that with me, right?"

Dancing…

Edyn hesitated, growing nervous just thinking about the party. Not realizing it, he was just staring at Serah instead of responding.

Always sensing a good opportunity for one of her playful quips, Serah tried to interrupt his trance. "What's wrong? Did I hypnotize you or something?" A smirk formed on her face as she slowly waved her hand in front of Edyn's eyes. *"You want to go with me… You want to go with me…"*

Edyn smiled and gave a light laugh at his friend's creativity. Finally, he responded in the only possible way he could after that: "Yeah, of course I'll go with you, Serah. That should be fun."

"I know!" she exclaimed, her eyes lighting up. "I can't wait!"

Serah studied Edyn for a few moments before refocusing and resuming in a more serious tone. "Now, why are you roaming the streets at this hour?"

What do I say?

2: SEASIDE

Over the past five months, Serah had become Edyn's closest friend, and someone he could open himself up to. He had told her that he couldn't remember much of his past before a few years ago, and while he suspected that Serah didn't fully believe him, she was understanding and accepting. However, he hadn't delved too deeply into it and still kept most things hidden from her.

He struggled to find the right words. "I had an appointment with a psychologist today. I was his last session of the day, and then just decided to hang out and walk around the Cove for a bit afterward. You know, to enjoy a little more of the summer weather while we still have it."

Serah's eyes widened. "Oh! I'm happy to hear that! I was wondering when you were going to see someone about what you told me. Don't worry, I won't ask you all about it now. But you know you can talk to me about it whenever you're ready."

"I know," Edyn said with a smile. "Thank you."

"You're too quiet to tell me a long story about all of that anyways!" Serah said playfully. "C'mon, let's head in."

Edyn followed Serah into their apartment building and up three flights to their apartment doors, which faced each other. Serah pulled out her keys. "I'm exhausted. Maybe tomorrow, if you'll be around, stop over, okay?"

As she looked at Edyn, he could see concern in her eyes. She dialed back her playfulness, allowing the natural sweet tone of her voice to shine through.

"I hope you're doing okay, Edyn. Let's talk tomorrow if you want, okay?" She yawned and smirked. "I'm not gonna last too much longer tonight, and I need to get my beauty sleep."

I'm probably the one who needs that tonight.

"Yeah, I'll see what you're up to tomorrow after my next appointment. Goodnight, Serah."

AFTERGLOW

Serah retreated to her apartment, and Edyn did the same. The inside was dark, with only the moonlight shining in through the windows. He turned on a lamp on the nearby end table and set down his keys. He felt happy to be back, and always felt so much happier when he was around Serah. Tonight, as usual, he seemed to forget about everything else when he was around her.

Edyn headed into his bathroom and rinsed his face in the sink. He stared at his reflection in the mirror. He didn't look great. His eyes looked dark, tired, and miserable—like he hadn't slept in days.

I look terrible.

Eager to shake off the effects of the day, he went to bed, hoping to sleep everything off. It didn't take long for his heavy eyes to drift off, and he soon fell into a deep sleep. Immediately, he began to dream.

He dreamed he was walking slowly through a dark expanse. Blue streaks of radiant energy shot forward through a black, formless path and all around the black and empty exterior. As Edyn advanced, he began to see what these streaks of light were leading him toward.

Ahead, he saw a white columned structure glowing radiantly. He felt as though he was being drawn to it. The structure was the centerpiece of the dream, and he focused on it as sparking electrical sounds rang in the distance.

As he drew closer to the hexagonal marble structure, he saw flowering vines climbing its columns. But as he neared, the image before him grew increasingly cloudy, fading away.

He thought he could see a pedestal in the center of the structure with something faintly glowing on top, but before he could get a closer look, the dream abruptly vanished, and he woke with a start.

He lay awake in bed, recalling the foggy remnants of the strange dream. But his calm state lasted only a few seconds before a bright

2: SEASIDE

flash appeared before his eyes and piercing electrical sounds rang through his ears.

A haunting voice echoed powerfully. Edyn was petrified, unable to catch his breath, frozen by fear.

> Do not be afraid.
> I can show you the way.

3
MEMORY'S CATARACT

Just don't think
There was anything you could have done
This is just how we have to end

We're going to be apart for a long time, but
If you get lost
Come back here
Just like we promised
I know you'll be able to find me

Keep me in your memories, Edyn
This is our goodbye
But I know I won't lose you forever, because
You'll still be where you've always been.

It's starting to happen all the time now. Twice yesterday after I left, and once again this morning. I know I told you it's been happening more frequently lately, which is why I came back to see you in the first place, but it was never like this."

Edyn was back in Raine's office the next day. He recounted how he'd broken down at the boardwalk and in the cemetery, and how he had experienced the visions more powerfully than usual.

"Each time now, I'm remembering just a little bit more. The woman who's speaking to me—I'm hearing her say more, further back in the conversation."

Edyn sat up straight in his chair, a distraught look covering his face.

"I feel so sad when it happens and when I hear her voice, and I don't even know why! I don't even know if it's real or not. How do I know if this vision, or memory, is even real?" He cast his gaze away. "Or if she's even real..." The sadness in his eyes grew more visible.

Raine struggled to find the right words to say, or an idea of what to do next. He adjusted his glasses, buying a few extra seconds to process the new information, and tried to stay confident to reassure him.

"I understand how you must feel. Yesterday was a deeply powerful experience for you, and I know you are confused." The answer to where to take the conversation next suddenly dawned on Raine, and he spoke with renewed confidence. "But I don't think it was a mere coincidence that so much happened after our session yesterday. I have reason to believe there is a justifiable cause."

Raine pressed on, and with even more conviction, added, "It is possible, with how we delved deeper into your memory of the hill yesterday, that we may have triggered your mind to remember even

3: MEMORY'S CATARACT

more about the experience. As you mentioned, you'd been having the vision more frequently lately anyways, so it's possible that we may now be accelerating that process. As to why you feel such sadness when it occurs, well, it's becoming clear that your emotions are deeply tied to whatever event occurred upon this hill."

Raine continued with poise and assertiveness, confidently clasping his hands together in his lap. "Something *must* have happened that day. And just as much as your mind closed everything off from you from that point on, to preserve itself and to protect you, it very well may now be beginning to want you to remember those hidden memories." He looked intently into Edyn's eyes, hoping that the importance of his next lines would sink in. "However, I believe it is partially up to you, as well. You have to want to remember, and if you do so, your mind may let you. I believe yesterday may have been the first time you've really *wanted* to remember."

Edyn started to feel as though he could finally relax. Raine's explanation made sense the more he thought it over. It did seem quite coincidental that the events of the previous day had happened just after his first session back, and it was true that Edyn hadn't talked openly about his vision to anyone before then. Still, after the disturbing night he'd had, he remained distraught.

"I still don't understand what the vision means," Edyn said. "I truly have no recollection, and—"

"Let us not refer to this as a 'vision' anymore," Raine interrupted, "but rather, let's assume that it is indeed a flashback. A memory, if you will, that was suppressed. From this point on, let's accept it as such, and refer to it only as that."

Edyn gave a silent nod as Raine expanded. "Your condition typically occurs as an emergency defense mechanism to prevent overwhelming trauma. Subconsciously, your mind decided to protect you from experiencing whatever was happening any further, and it eliminated the experience altogether from your memories. It's as if your mind had constructed impenetrable ramparts to protect you. A shadow was cast over those memories, shrouding them from you. A fog, cast across your neural pathways. But those memories—they are still in there, somewhere."

The doctor stood, crossed his office to the water cooler, and poured a cup of water. "The fact that you are remembering more and more of this memory is a very encouraging sign for us, actually." He handed Edyn the cup of water. "Now please, try to accept this memory for what it is, and let's talk more about what you're feeling during it."

Edyn took a slow sip from the cup and set it on the end table next to his chair, avoiding the overreach of the fern. "Like I was saying," he said, "the past few times I've experienced it, it's like it's going back further and further toward the beginning of the conversation each time it starts. But the woman in it—I still can't see her at all. I can only hear her voice."

"Ah, yes," Raine said, pouring himself a cup of water. "And from what you've told me, she calls you by your name." He took a sip. "What else does she say to you?"

A knot formed in Edyn's throat. "She's saying goodbye to me. For good." He paused to collect himself before continuing. "She has a sadness in her voice. Almost a sense of dread. It's such a dark atmosphere. She's telling me that this is how we have to end—with this goodbye."

Edyn shifted in his chair and spun his eyes toward Raine. "I know what you're thinking. And I guess it's possible it could be a memory of a final goodbye with a past love, but I just don't understand how I wouldn't remember her, then. She sounds my

3: MEMORY'S CATARACT

age, but who knows if that's even who she was. She could have been a relative, or a friend."

"Very peculiar..." Raine thought aloud, scratching his chin and gazing upward. "We won't jump to any conclusions just yet, but you may already be on the right track with the meaning of this memory. I believe there is still quite a bit more to the story to uncover along with her goodbye, but I want you to know that even a loved one being lost has indeed led to minor cases of your condition. It is amazing how much our emotions, and with that, our *minds*, can become tied to another person."

Raine stood, seemingly shifting his thoughts as he went to his bookshelf and skimmed over some of the books. "But that's enough discussion on the memory for today. I don't want to overdo it." He turned back to Edyn. "I want our sessions to be open conversations about all things. We won't solely be discussing your condition or memory. There is so much more around all this that I want to help you understand, and I'm going to try my best to open your mind above all else, as that is the most important thing that will help us. Once you can accept the realities of some of the unusual things around us, you may start to realize your condition isn't so strange after all." Raine chuckled to himself. "And what a strange world it is that we live in!"

Raine expected some sort of response from Edyn but quickly noticed his patient wasn't all there. "Is everything okay?" Raine asked.

Edyn was lost in thought. "Is it possible to have feelings for someone you've never seen before?"

Raine didn't immediately respond, trying to formulate an answer to the question. Before he could think of something to say, Edyn continued.

"I know it's that I just can't remember her, but right now, it's almost like I'm feeling something for someone within a dream. Someone who doesn't even exist."

"My friend, yes!" Raine quickly interjected. "Of course it is possible! I think the fact that you are feeling these feelings, proves she does exist!" He glanced briefly at his bookshelf and smiled. "A dream, you say? What a great word you chose to use. It is possible for you to have these feelings for someone within a dream. Dreams, memories—they are related experiences."

Raine paced around the room as he explained further.

"Your mind and your soul are the parts of you experiencing these things. And there is so much hidden within us that we cannot measure—the special parts of us that are taking part in the dream, or memory. Whether it's your recurring flashback, or simply a nightly dream, the deepest parts of you are what's connected to them. These aspects of you—your mind, your soul, your *you*—these are invisible and unmeasurable things. So we can't dismiss something we feel for someone that we simply cannot measure, or in this case, see." Raine seemed to get lost in his thoughts for a moment. "We can remain connected to others sometimes, somewhere, in a special place, unseen…"

Raine sat back down and refocused, his gaze firm.

"Now, let me ask you this: Have you ever awakened from a dream and experienced yourself still dreaming for a few seconds? Still seeing an image from the dream, or feeling something for someone within the dream, even though you are awake and aware? A dream that just lingers a bit longer than it should?"

Edyn nodded, and replied, without much conviction, "Yeah, I think that might have happened to me a few times."

"Exactly! Now, how can we explain that? And who's to say this couldn't happen to someone for even a bit longer? When you are breaking down and experiencing your memory, it could be that you

3: MEMORY'S CATARACT

are experiencing something similar to this phenomenon, while you are wide awake."

Raine hoped Edyn would understand what he was getting at, but Edyn remained silent with a confused look on his face, not quite sure of the point.

"You see," Raine expanded, his voice resolute, "the fact that you are having the same memory, or dream, we can call it, and are recalling more and more about it each time, already puts you in better shape to figure out its meaning than the rest of the dreamers out there. You're even experiencing a very real feeling during it. Your mind is making more sense of this than you realize. The answer is in there, and it's trying to come out."

"Maybe you're right," Edyn said, but there was little confidence in his voice. Suddenly, he straightened, as if struck by another thought. "Something you said, though, about a dream that lingers a bit while you're awake. There's something else I've been experiencing that I haven't told you about yet."

Edyn thought back on the times when he heard that other strange voice speaking to him after his flashback had ended—specifically, the two frightening times it happened yesterday, including after his dream. "Sometimes, just after I experience the memory, I hear a *different* voice speaking to me while I'm coming back to my senses."

Edyn recalled the intense fear he'd felt yesterday at the sound of the voice, and how much more real it felt than times before. "It used to happen only once in a while, right after my memory had ended, or maybe at other times too. But it was always so faint, and I never really thought much of it. But yesterday—yesterday it was a lot different. I could clearly hear what the voice was saying, and it was all so *real*." He cast his eyes downward as the terror he'd felt the day before gripped him.

"I heard these electrical sounds when it happened, and then afterward, all I could see was darkness."

Raine fell silent, seemingly caught off-guard by this new revelation. He didn't quite know what to say, and he again adjusted his glasses to buy himself some time. He could sense Edyn's fear.

"Now," Raine spoke hesitantly, "you say this is a different voice? Can you describe what it sounds like? Is it like the other voice?"

Edyn immediately shook his head. "No—not at all. It's something else. Much different."

Completely different.

"The voice sounds male, but something is *very* different about it. It's so powerful, and has an engulfing energy. It's hard to describe, but it's almost like I'm not actually hearing the words spoken to me. It's more like they're echoing all around and within me."

Raine gave himself a few moments to process the new information before replying. "Hmm, it's possible your mind may be in some state of confusion as you are coming out of your memory." He then continued more assuredly. "Since your mind really does go somewhere else when you experience your memory, there's definitely the chance of experiencing something that seems odd as you are 'snapping back into it,' for lack of a better phrase."

With a jolt, Edyn quickly interjected, "You don't understand, though. It wasn't something like waking up from a dream. It was so real." Edyn again felt the terror he'd experienced yesterday crawling inside of him. "There was something so familiar about the voice, like I've known it for a long time. And the things he was saying were, just, so strange…"

"What did he say, Edyn?"

Sadness descended upon Edyn, replacing the fear, as he recalled

3: MEMORY'S CATARACT

what the voice had said. "After my memory ended, he basically questioned how I don't remember that day, and stated that *he* remembers it, almost mocking me. As if whoever he is was there that day." He cast his eyes downward dejectedly.

"I'm sorry," Raine said. "I can tell this is difficult, and I know it seems what you heard was odd. But I don't want you to worry so much about this other voice you've been hearing." Then, with more reassurance in his voice, Raine continued with what he undoubtedly believed to be the explanation. "But I think what you heard is actually quite common in cases such as yours. Remember, there is a part of you that remembers everything. We're just trying to get that part to come back out and take over again. It can be difficult to consider, but I think that you may be telling yourself that you remember that day, and are asking yourself how you don't. Does that make sense?"

I don't think so.

"It does, I guess," Edyn hesitantly replied, telling the doctor what he wanted to hear. Even though he completely understood where Raine was coming from, deep down, he knew there was something more about that mysterious voice, and he knew Raine's explanation certainly wasn't it. It was something else entirely.

As he thought on it, one of the pieces of artwork on Raine's wall caught Edyn's eye. It depicted a white room with a spiral of colors approaching the viewer. As he stared on expressionlessly, Raine tried to interrupt his trance. "By the way, how have your headaches been today?"

Edyn was mesmerized by the image before him, feeling as if he were chasing a fleeting thought. "Oh, they're about the same," he replied sluggishly.

He remained entirely transfixed by the painting. Something about the spiral of colors made him feel something deeply familiar.

Meanwhile, impossibly, the spiral began to move, extending outward from the frame, reaching toward him.

The terrifying voice came again, reverberating in Edyn's head, and confusing his fragile mind.

> Yes... open your mind.
> Do not resist me.
> You cannot escape my reach.

4
SHIMMER

"Edyn, are you ready?"

Edyn jumped up, startled by the sound of knocking at his door and the muffled sound of Serah's voice coming from the other side.

Ready for what?

He hesitantly approached the door, a terrible feeling developing inside that he was forgetting something. He paused a moment before reluctantly opening the door, feeling like he was about to let his friend down—although for what, exactly, he wasn't sure.

The door swung open and Edyn caught himself completely transfixed by the radiant gaze of the woman looking back at him.

She's so beautiful.

Serah was dressed in a long, form-fitting black dress, her wavy brown hair flowing down over it. She wore gold earrings that sparkled in the light, perfectly paired with her usual necklace and charm, which hung loosely from her neck.

"Serah, you look…" Edyn looked into her warm amber eyes and felt unable to speak.

Serah studied him from head to toe, and a confused but playful look crossed her face. "I know you're not exactly on the cutting edge of style or anything, but I also know you have a little more sense than this." She looked back up at him, her eyes showing a hint of disappointment. "You forgot, didn't you?"

Forgot?

"I..." Edyn tried to remember what he was forgetting.

"It's Saturday night," Serah prompted, trying to jog Edyn's memory. "My end-of-summer work party at the museum?"

All at once it hit Edyn, and he got a terrible feeling in the pit of his stomach. "Serah, I'm so sorry! I completely forgot!" He cast his eyes down in shame, fully expecting Serah's disappointment. But when he looked up, she was smiling.

"That's okay," she said, walking past him and into his apartment. "I'll wait 'til you're ready." She spun back around to face him, a smirk on her face. "You're not getting out of this *that* easy."

"Are you sure? I'm not even dressed or anything," Edyn said.

Serah took a seat on his couch. "It's okay, I'll wait." Then, gazing straight ahead with a more serious look on her face, she said, "Just so you're there with me."

Edyn nodded. "Okay. I'll try to hurry up."

He went into his bedroom and felt a jolt of panic as he tried to find the right thing to wear. Serah was all dressed up, and he knew it was because this was something she'd been looking forward to. He went through his clean clothes and put on a pair of dark-blue slacks, a gray collared shirt, and paired them with a brown leather belt and matching brown dress shoes. Then he ducked into the bathroom to freshen up and comb his hair before presenting himself to Serah.

He examined himself in the mirror.

Not bad, given the circumstances.

He turned to go, but Serah was already standing in the

4: SHIMMER

bathroom doorway. "You look so handsome."

Immediately, a nervousness came over Edyn. This was the first time Serah had said something like that to him. He stumbled a bit internally before responding, "Thanks. So do you."

"So do I? I look handsome?" Serah laughed and tugged his hand as to speed up the process. "C'mon, silly man. We're already going to be late."

Before he knew it, Edyn was following Serah to her car in the parking lot. "I'll drive," she said. "I know the way." She got in and frantically began to clear his seat off and throw some things into the back. "I know, I know, it's a mess."

She seemed nervous, and she gave a short laugh when Edyn got in and she saw how cramped he was.

"I guess this little car is a bit too small for a tall guy like you," she said. She started the car and smiled at him before taking off. "Oh, well. Guess you're going to have to deal with it tonight."

As she pulled out, Serah rolled down the windows and popped a CD into the car stereo. "All I Want" by Toad The Wet Sprocket began to play. Edyn didn't notice the longing smile Serah cast his way when it started.

They drove east out of Riverwood Cove toward downtown and Edyn felt content, enjoying this chance to free his mind from the more serious things he'd been dealing with lately. He listened to the song's soothing melody as he stared out the window at the early autumnal scenery, wind blowing through his long hair.

He glanced over at Serah and saw that she looked apprehensive. When she noticed him looking at her, she gave a hesitant smile. "I'm a little nervous, you know?"

"Nervous? *You?*" Edyn couldn't believe this bubbly, quick-witted girl, who never seemed shy in any situation, could ever feel that way.

"Yeah. I hide it well. I *am* really excited, but I'm…" She exhaled. "I'm just glad you're here with me."

"Me too," Edyn said, offering her assurance.

They pulled into the parking lot of the museum, and Edyn peered up at the building as he stepped out of the car. It was crafted in light sandstone and had gargoyle statues perched at its top corners. The glow of fading streaks of sunlight shone across the outer surfaces of the statues. It was nearly half past seven, and even though the sky was still well lit, sunset was only minutes away.

Still gazing upward, Edyn began to walk toward the front door, but Serah stopped him. "C'mon, we're gonna go in a different way. I want to avoid the main entrance and drawing attention."

She led Edyn to a small door at the back of the building. They entered and advanced into a side hallway. Moving down the hallway, they came to a large gallery and went inside. Many of the pieces in the exhibit were covered in cloth, and some of them were marked.

"We really shouldn't be in these galleries right now," Serah said. "They have a lot of work this weekend getting the fall exhibits ready for next week."

After making their way through the gallery, Edyn began to hear the bassy sounds of music playing. He looked to his right into another open gallery. Most of the pieces in it were of symbols. One in particular caught his eye. He recognized it.

Intrigued, Edyn stopped and squinted his eyes to examine it further, but Serah caught him by the arm before he could get a closer look. "This way. We're already late."

They came to an intersection where the muffled sound of music grew louder. A few people were heading through large double doors next to a check-in desk down the hall to the right. Flashing lights crept from the other side of the doors.

4: SHIMMER

"That's the main entrance to the dining hall," Serah said. "Let's just keep heading this way and go in a side door to avoid it. We can sneak in and try to pretend we weren't late."

"Whatever you say," Edyn said.

Farther down the hallway, they came to the side door. Serah, trying to overcome her nervousness, took a deep breath. "Alright, let's do this," she said and opened the door discreetly, allowing them both to silently creep in.

A wave of loud pop music hit them as soon as they stepped inside. Scanning the hall and the people mingling about, Edyn grew nervous too. The hall itself was dimly lit, but there were many colorful, flashing lights coinciding with the rhythm of the music. "Well, I guess 1994 hasn't gotten enough Ace of Base yet," Serah sarcastically remarked.

Quietly closing the door they'd come through, she began to say, "I think we successfully snuck—" but before she could finish, a loud voice exclaimed, "Hey! There you two are!"

A woman with long blonde hair and an overly strong scent of perfume grabbed Serah from behind and forcefully spun her around for a full embrace. "I was wondering where you were! Did you just try to sneak in here?"

"No..." Serah smiled, then added, "Maybe." The two shared a quick laugh together, and Serah began the introductions. "Edyn, this is Kristen. Kristen, this is my—"

"Boyfriend?" Kristen playfully quipped.

"My *friend*, Edyn," Serah quickly corrected.

Now uncomfortable, Edyn managed to fake a smile. "It's nice to meet you, Kristen."

"You too, Serah's *friend*," she replied with a mischievous smile.

"Kristen is another curatorial assistant here at the museum," Serah said.

To this, Kristen added in a humorously dramatic tone, "Yes, yes. Curators by day, drunks by night!" She took a look around the hall. "Hey, sometimes it can be tough being trapped in these beautifully peaceful walls all day. Time to get out and let loose a little!"

Edyn gave her a perplexed look. "Get out? Aren't you technically still within those walls right now?"

Serah smiled to herself, being careful not to let Kristen see. A few moments of silence ensued while Kristen seemed to be debating how to respond. Edyn hoped he hadn't accidentally offended someone he'd just met.

Finally, Kristen responded with a smile. "I like him. He can hang, I guess." Serah's smile grew larger, and Kristen continued, "Speaking of letting loose. You two should go grab a drink at our makeshift bar over there."

"Good idea!" Serah said and motioned for Edyn to follow her.

There were forty or so people mingling throughout the hall. Some sat at two-person bistro tables with food, and others held drinks as they moved about, socializing. Edyn saw a few people dancing and grew worried.

Isn't it kind of early for that?

They made their way over to the cafeteria area where a woman behind a tall wooden table was tending and serving drinks. There were a few wine and liquor bottles on the table, as well as beer stocked in the drink cooler behind her.

As they approached, Serah locked eyes with the woman, and both seemed excited to see one another. "Edyn," Serah said, "this is Dana. She has gracefully volunteered her services to be our bartender for the night."

"Hey, girl!" Dana said. She was dressed in her own style, seeming to rebel against getting all fancied-up like the rest of the

4: SHIMMER

crowd. She had short black hair with a dark-blue beanie overtop and a long-sleeved top to match. Edyn appreciated her style and attitude. "That's right! I'm your fancy bartender for the night. You name it, you got it! Well, as long as you mean beer or one type of cheap wine, and if you promise to keep your mixed drink requests simple for me."

"I'll just stick with that delicious merlot you have there," Serah said.

As Dana poured Serah her drink, she perked her ears up, taking notice of the song that began playing. " 'Regulate'? At a museum party? Gotta admit, didn't see that one coming." She handed Serah the glass of wine and turned to Edyn. "And what would you like, sir?"

"What kinds of beer do you have?" Edyn asked.

"Kinds? What kind of establishment do you think this is?" She handed Edyn a bottle of the only beer they had and then urged the two to go have some fun.

As they walked away, Serah motioned to the appetizer table nearby. "We're going to need energy for dancing!"

Dancing...

Edyn reluctantly followed her to the appetizer table and scanned the spread of food. "Not bad for our little museum, huh?" Serah remarked, picking up a handful of cubed cheese and crackers.

"No, not at all," Edyn said. "This whole thing is really cool, actually. And I like all your friends."

Serah smiled to herself as she finished filling her small plate with food, then led Edyn to a nearby table to sit together.

"Thanks again for coming as my guest," Serah said.

"Of course!" Edyn replied, as he took note of the typical dance music playing.

AFTERGLOW

I don't think I'm gonna be hearing any Gin Blossoms tonight.

They sat at the table with their food and drinks and talked until the moment Edyn had been dreading inevitably occurred. A new song began to play, and Serah jumped up out of her seat. "I love this song!" She turned to Edyn. "Shall we?"

What do I do?

"I'm..." Edyn hesitantly replied, "not really much of a dancer, you know?"

She laughed. "Well, I must say, that's not too shocking. C'mon, it'll be fun! It's just me. Are you sure?"

Edyn chose his words carefully. "I mean, I'd love to dance with you, and all. It's just not really my thing. You should go, though!"

Serah looked disappointed but understood. "Be back in a bit!" she said and scurried off to join a small group already on the dance floor. Edyn sat at the table and watched her.

She looks so beautiful tonight.

From the dance floor, Serah locked eyes with him. She smiled, but there was a longing expression on her face.

Just then, a sharp pain shot through Edyn's head. Something about the way Serah was looking at him reminded him of the way someone else used to look at him. And the way she looked in that black dress...

Edyn's vision flickered, piercing electrical sounds rang, and the image of Serah morphed into a blurry image of another woman.

But before Edyn could even process what was happening, everything returned to normal, as if nothing had happened. Only a stray sparkling purple leaf, which had seemingly come out of nowhere, fell before his face from above. Fascinated, he squinted at it, but the moment it landed on the floor, it vanished.

Edyn sat motionless, momentarily frozen by what he'd just seen. Feeling that he needed to go somewhere else to clear his

4: SHIMMER

mind, he started to stand when a hand appeared, sliding another bottle of beer in front of him.

"Here, I noticed you were running low," Dana said.

"Thanks," Edyn replied as he tried to gather himself. He turned back to the dance floor and saw Serah dancing with another man. His spirits plummeted.

I should have gone out there. Why am I like this?

Dana, immediately picking up on the situation, explained, "Don't worry about him. He's been trying for years. Ugh! It makes me want to vomit."

"Oh... I... I wasn't..." Edyn stammered.

"Hey, you don't gotta explain to me, friend. She's a great girl. The best there is, actually." She paused, looking out at Serah. "Just hasn't always had the best of luck." She turned her focus back to Edyn. "But anyways, I'm away from my post, and duty calls. Enjoy!" With that, Dana hurried back to tend bar, leaving Edyn alone again.

Taking a look around, he saw several people coming in and out through a set of large glass doors at the far end of the hall which appeared to lead outside.

Maybe I'll just head out there for a bit.

Edyn was careful to sneak past the dance floor without Serah seeing him. On his way, he passed a small group of people and overheard their conversation as he walked by.

"Did I tell you that I got a job down at the Cove with that old drilling company that's reopening?"

"You did? Aren't they the ones that got shut down a few years ago due to that bad accident?"

"Yeah. But I think they got everything in order now, and the starting pay is just too good to pass up."

Edyn ignored the conversation and moved past the group. A

familiar face caught him trying to make his escape. "Hi, again! You're going the wrong way! All the fun is in here!" Edyn smiled as he made his way past Kristen, acknowledging her comment but not wanting to get stuck in conversation.

Reaching the glass doors, Edyn pulled them open and stepped through. Instantly, a whiff of the cool mid-September evening breeze hit him. He walked out onto a stone-paved area toward a railing where a few other people were also getting some air.

On the other side of the railing was a small courtyard with a white stone fountain in the middle, surrounded by colorful flowers. It was pitch black outside but the courtyard was well lit, and the moonlight shining down from above added to its glow, giving the setting a serene appearance. Edyn rested up against the railing and looked out, trying to free his mind and enjoy the scenery.

This is more like it.

He took in the calm, only the sounds of the fountain and a few soft-spoken conversations nearby filling the air. Before long, he heard the doors behind him opening. The music swelled, and a familiar voice spoke, "Thought I might find you out here." Before Edyn could turn, Serah came up alongside him and rested against the railing.

"Yeah," Edyn said, "I thought I'd just step out for a bit."

Serah touched his shoulder. "Thanks again for coming with me tonight, Edyn. I know this really isn't your type of scene. It means a lot to me that you came."

"Of course, Serah."

She looked out at the moonlit courtyard. "It's such a nice night, isn't it?"

Edyn followed her gaze. "Yeah, it really is."

"It's so beautiful here, and especially at this time of year." She took in the view. "Makes you wonder how all of this is even here."

4: SHIMMER

At those words, a strange feeling came over Edyn. He turned to Serah. "What do you mean?"

"This town, silly. It's just so peaceful here, and then we also have the beauty of the Cove not too far away. We're really lucky, you know. And somehow, not too many people seem to know about it."

Edyn nodded in agreement. They stood together and chatted until the temperature fell and the breeze began to pick up. "Don't you want to go back inside with your friends?" Edyn asked. "I don't want to make you feel like you have to stay out here with—"

"It's okay," Serah said, looking up into his eyes. "I'd rather be here with you." It looked as if there was something more she wanted to say, but couldn't. Instead, she wrapped her arms around Edyn's left arm and rested her head against it. Edyn was caught off-guard, but enjoyed the moment with her as they gazed out to the tranquil courtyard.

The wind became fierce, and Edyn saw storm clouds approaching. "Well, I think we'd better head in regardless. Looks like rain is coming." He also felt a strong headache coming on.

Serah quickly removed herself from him, seemingly flustered. "Yeah, you're right. Let's head back in."

As the two turned, the faint sound of thunder in the distance became audible. And at that very instant, just as Edyn saw their reflection on the glass doors, his vision again flickered.

He tried to shake it off, but his surroundings suddenly disappeared. All that remained were their reflections on the glass doors, surrounded by black emptiness. Edyn stood in shock as Serah's reflection blurred and began to morph into the form of another woman. Electrical sounds pierced his ears. The dark and formless figure grew more vivid as the sounds increased in volume, but just as it was starting to come to fruition, it all vanished just as quickly as it had come. Everything was back to normal. Everything except for the headache, which had doubled in intensity.

Edyn tried to fight through it as they headed back inside, but the pain rapidly intensified to the point that it stopped him in his tracks. He put his hand to his head, bracing himself.

"What's wrong? Are you okay?" Serah asked.

"Yeah, it's just a headache. I'm okay," Edyn groggily replied. "But I might want to head back now. I don't want to put you out, so I can ask around—"

"No, don't worry about it!" Serah quickly interjected. "It's just a short drive. I can take you home, and I could even come right back here for the last hour or so. Really, it's no big deal."

"Thanks…"

…*and sorry.*

It was raining heavily when Serah dropped Edyn off at their apartment building. He walked up the few flights of stairs to the third floor, his headache intensifying further. Approaching his apartment door, he looked out the large window at the end of the hall spanning from floor to ceiling. There was a storm raging outside in full force, and as he watched the falling rain, he thought he heard something coming from behind him. He spun around, but nothing was there.

Edyn tried to brush it off, and opened his door. Once inside, he slipped off his shoes, went to the kitchen, and poured himself a glass of water. Outside, the thunder was booming. He looked out his window and saw bright flashes of lightning filling the dark sky.

As he took a drink, he turned and viewed himself in the small mirror over the sink. More bolts of lightning struck, illuminating the kitchen. But as frightening as the lightning was, it didn't compare to the horrifying image that appeared before him. With

4: SHIMMER

each flash and crack of lightning, he saw a terrifying figure revealed in the mirror taking the place of his reflection—a blue sideways spiral of flowing energy. Deafening electrical sounds rang as the blue spiral pulsated and intensified to the point where Edyn could almost feel it. Gripped with fear, his wavering hand dropped the glass and it shattered in the sink.

> I've been trying to reach you.
> There was an accident.
> You made an error in judgment.
> I can help you find her.

5
FRAGMENTS

Edyn hit the ground hard and passed out. Lying weak and powerless on his kitchen floor, he again experienced the familiar memory within the depths of his fractured mind—this time recalling even more.

It began with Edyn approaching the hill instead of already sitting at the top. He stepped through waves of tall grass on either side of him, winding up a beaten-down path toward the top of the moonlit hill. As he drew closer, he heard the waves of the sea crashing hard into the rocks below. Nearing the top, something came into view.

The dark, blurry figure of a woman stood at the top of the hill, facing away from him, and gazing upward at the gigantic moon overhead. It glowed brightly, its light illuminating the waving blades of grass at the summit and the rippling waves of the crashing sea below.

Edyn reached the top of the hill and sat beside the mysterious figure. Immediately, she turned to look at him. To his shock, the blurred figure had no discernible face. Still, he made out her dark attire and the dark hair surrounding her formless face.

She looked downward at the rocks below and then sat beside

him, her blurred form mysteriously shifting through the otherwise vivid memory.

    She began to speak, initially with only faint, muffled echoes able to be heard. But eventually, her familiar voice faded in and became fully audible.

> I'm sorry, but
> I have to leave you now
> It's all my fault, so
> Just don't think
> There was anything you could have done
> This is just how we have to end
>
> We're going to be apart for a long time, but
> If you get lost
> Come back here
> Just like we promised
> I know you'll be able to find me
>
> Keep me in your memories, Edyn
> This is our goodbye
> But I know I won't lose you forever, because
> You'll still be where you've always been

    Just as the last line was spoken, the entire setting began to swirl around Edyn, while loud electrical surges rang in his ears.

    "You'll still be where you've always been." Her haunting last words echoed in Edyn's ears as the memory faded.

5: FRAGMENTS

But just before it vanished, the woman's formless face flickered in rapid succession, a clear view of her face coming through. And in those tiny moments, Edyn thought he caught a fleeting glimpse of what she looked like. But it was only enough to torment him further. Before he knew it, both the memory and the woman's face disappeared, and another came into view.

"Edyn! Edyn! Are you alright?!"

Huh?

"Serah?"

Serah had both hands on Edyn's shoulders and was gently shaking him awake.

"What are you doing here?" Edyn asked, opening his eyes and gradually coming to his senses.

"I think I should be asking you that question," Serah replied as it dawned on Edyn that he was lying on his kitchen floor. "Are you alright?" He winced, and Serah continued. "Your door was open when I came back home. I knocked to see if everything was okay, but didn't hear anything. Sorry to intrude, but I'm really glad I did. You were passed out cold here when I walked in. Are you okay?"

She helped Edyn sit up, and he tried to shake off his grogginess. "Yeah. I mean, I think so."

Serah saw that her hand had slipped into Edyn's as he sat up, and she quickly pulled it away. To distract, and to lighten the mood, she said, "What's going on here? Did you have one too many beers at the party and decide to take a nap on your kitchen floor?"

Edyn gave a light laugh, but when he tried to think about what had happened, he couldn't remember. All he recalled was dropping his glass in the sink just as a flash of lightning struck.

Then it hit him.

"I've been trying to reach you."

A jolt of fear shot through him as he recalled the terrifying image he'd seen in the mirror and the strange words that were spoken to him.

Was it just my imagination?

He knew he couldn't explain what had happened. He didn't even understand it himself. "I really don't know," he said. "I must have gotten lightheaded or something. The last thing I remember was dropping my glass in the sink. I don't remember much after that."

"Hmm," Serah hummed to herself as she stood and took a look in the sink. "You are correct, detective!" She turned back to Edyn with her hands on her hips. "I think this case is complete. You know, you may have a future in this field!" She extended her hand to help Edyn up. "Now go relax on the couch and let me clean up this mess for you."

"You really don't have to, but thanks." Edyn steadied himself and headed into his living room while Serah cleaned up the broken glass. He smiled as he moved past her, knowing how lucky he was that she had shown up, and how much better she always seemed to make things.

As he sat on his couch, he recalled something else: what he had seen at the end of the memory. He couldn't get the image of the woman's blurred form out of his head, nor the frightening sight of her flickering face just before Serah had woken him up.

Who are you?

"You're lucky, you know," Edyn heard Serah say from the kitchen, interrupting his thoughts. "This glass could have broken on the floor and you could have cut yourself up really bad falling on it." She disposed of the rest of the broken glass and walked over to Edyn, casting a glance out the window. "Some storm, huh?"

Outside, the rain was still falling heavily, although the lightning

5: FRAGMENTS

and thunder seemed to have finally dissipated.

Serah sat on the couch with Edyn but kept a space between them. "So you've been getting lightheaded lately, is that it?" She asked. "What about that headache earlier tonight?"

Immediately, Edyn felt uneasy. As good as he was at keeping things hidden, he wasn't good at lying. He hesitated before finally deciding to open up to her. "You know how I've told you before that I can't remember much of my past?"

Serah nodded.

"Well, it's not just that." Edyn shifted in his seat. "I know it sounds crazy, but I can't remember *anything* about my past prior to about three years ago. That's the main reason I'm seeing the doctor I used to see again. But that's not the only reason. I haven't been completely honest with you. I've been... *seeing* things, too."

"Seeing things?"

Edyn nodded. "There's this recurring vision or, memory, of me on top of a hill that I've always had. It just comes out of nowhere. And lately, it's been happening a lot more, and feeling a lot more real. That's what my psychologist and I are working to figure out. The meaning behind this memory, and why it keeps coming back to me. And I've seen other strange things lately too..."

Edyn cast his eyes downward and shook his head.

"I don't know. It's hard to make sense of it all right now, but earlier tonight, the last thing I remember before you found me lying on the floor, was seeing something strange in my kitchen mirror. Something that wasn't there."

"Couldn't" have been there...

Serah could tell Edyn was troubled. "Edyn..." She moved closer to him. "You know I'm here for you, right? I had no idea all this other stuff was going on too. You know you can always talk to me, and you don't have to keep anything hidden from me, okay?

I hope I've made you feel that way these past few months."

You have.

"But I know some of these things are difficult to talk about. And believe me, it was difficult for me to understand your condition when you first told me about it. But I believed you then, and I believe you now."

A look of concern crossed her face.

"But I do hope your doctor figures out something soon. It was scary seeing you on the floor like that tonight." She stood and went to the window, looking out at the rain. "You know, if it makes you feel any better, I haven't been completely honest with you, either."

"What do you mean?"

Serah took a deep breath. "Well, for starters, my real name isn't Serah. It's Micaela." She paused, watching the rainfall, her face filling with sadness. "Serah was my mother's name." She swallowed. "Well, it's my middle name, too." She walked back toward Edyn, sat on the couch, and tried to collect herself. "When we first met and you helped me move some things, that woman you saw in the pictures that fell out of a box... that was my mother, Serah."

Her eyes welled with tears as she tried to fight the knot that was forming in her throat.

"But that was from before I ever got to meet her. You see, she passed away during my childbirth. There were unusual complications with my birth that were never able to be explained. The doctors said it was nearly impossible that I made it out alive. They told my dad... they told him that I was a miracle."

Edyn didn't quite know what to say. "Serah, I'm so sorry. I..."

Serah continued as if she hadn't heard him. " 'The gift from God.' That's what my dad used to always call me when I was young, and that's why he named me Micaela. But it doesn't feel like

5: FRAGMENTS

I was much of a gift with what happened and all. And once I was old enough to learn the truth, I made the decision to go by my mother's name from then on. To carry on her memory, I guess." She cast her gaze down and sniffed. "It's weird, you know—how much love I felt and still feel for this woman. I've never even met her." She looked up at Edyn, tears streaming down her face. "How can I feel that way about someone I've never met before?"

Edyn felt a deep connection with her in this moment. Her feelings were something he knew all too well. "There's nothing weird about that at all," he said reassuringly, scooting closer to her. "Especially with someone like that who you're obviously connected to. Her light—it still shines within you."

"You think so?"

Edyn finally acknowledged the tears sliding down Serah's face. He handed her a nearby box of tissues. "Of course. Things like that, they don't make much sense because we can't see them. But they're still real." He moved even closer to Serah as she blew her nose, her face streaked with tears.

"My real name—it's a lot to live up to with its meaning and all." She began wiping away her tears. "My dad was never quite the same after I was born and my mom passed, or so my family has told me. He's since passed too, but I never really felt like I lived up to his expectations. Or that maybe I wasn't good enough to help him fill the void of what he lost. Deep down I've always felt, in a way, that it was my fault for my mother's death." She turned to Edyn with a distraught look on her face. "How am I supposed to live with that?"

He put his arm around her to comfort her. "Now stop that. You know, of course, it wasn't your fault. You shouldn't feel like that."

For a moment, it felt like Serah seemed to like his embrace, and she began to tilt her head as if she were going to rest it on Edyn's shoulder. But she quickly stopped herself and pulled away. She stood, seemingly flustered.

"Sorry," she said, "I didn't mean to tell you so much. It just kind of happened. This wasn't even supposed to be about me, was it?" She gave a light anxious laugh and turned away. "Sorry. I shouldn't have told you all that."

After a few moments, she turned back to Edyn, expecting some sort of reassurance, but none came. Instead, she saw a distant expression on his face as he stared blankly downward.

"Edyn! Edyn! What's wrong?!" she asked. But Edyn's mind was elsewhere.

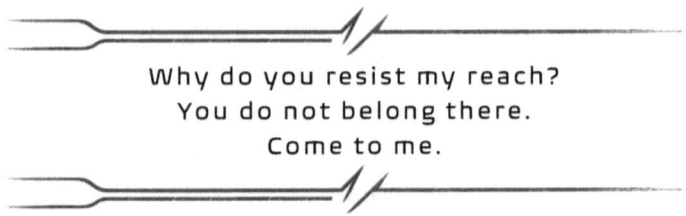

Why do you resist my reach?
You do not belong there.
Come to me.

Edyn's mind drifted off to the same place in the dream he'd had two nights earlier. Once again, he was slowly walking through a dark black expanse. Blue streaks of light shot rapidly around the black and formless void surrounding him, their radiant energy lighting the way forward.

Edyn was drawn to the white columned structure ahead emitting a bright glow. It was small in stature, hexagonal, with six stone columns supporting a small roof overhead. As he drew closer, he saw flowering vines growing around its marbled pillars.

Finally, he reached the structure, and a white stone pedestal was presented in its center. Piercing electrical sounds rang loudly.

He stepped inside and up to the waist-high pedestal. The blue

5: FRAGMENTS

streaks of light connected to the pedestal and ran up its sides, giving it a blue glow of energy and power.

Floating above the pedestal was a golden glowing object, but before Edyn could take a closer look, the dream began to fade, and his curious eyes quickly moved to an inscription on the top of the pedestal. He squinted, and just before the dream abruptly vanished, read the words *Ab Aeterno*.

6
COGNITION

It was inevitable
I had to try something
To see if we could have a future

I'm sorry, but
I have to leave you now
It's all my fault, so
Just don't think
There was anything you could have done
This is just how we have to end

We're going to be apart for a long time, but
If you get lost
Come back here
Just like we promised
I know you'll be able to find me

AFTERGLOW

> Keep me in your memories, Edyn
> This is our goodbye
> But I know I won't lose you forever, because
> You'll still be where you've always been

"I think I saw her Saturday night, just for a moment."

"You did?!"

Edyn nodded. "She was actually there this time. At least, I think so." Edyn described the woman's blurred, formless, unsettling appearance, and how the scene took shape with him approaching the hill. He didn't disclose that he'd passed out beforehand, nor what he saw in the mirror in the moments preceding.

"My word," Raine said, trying to hide his shock. "Your mind really *is* wanting you to remember."

"I just wish I knew how long before three years ago this memory was. It would make it so much easier."

"I know," Raine said, his voice comforting. "It is hard, because we don't know whether this is just a stray memory from some point in time of your past, or if it was from just before the onset of your condition. However, I'm starting to believe it is probably the latter."

Raine shifted his thoughts. "But let's not get too hung up on trying to determine when exactly this memory took place. What's more important is for us to keep unlocking more of it. Memories are one of the most mysterious and often misunderstood aspects of our minds, and to a large extent, our entire existence." He gave a chuckle. "Naturally, one of my favorite topics!"

Raine calmly placed his hands in his lap, leaned toward Edyn, and expanded in a confident, assured tone. "We don't have it right.

6: COGNITION

The way we think of them, that is. Memories aren't just things from the past that we think about. Memories are real, and they make all of us who we are. We live in memories. We carry them with us. They determine how we think, act, and make decisions. We *are* memories. We are someone *else's* memory. There are even times when we 'carry on' the memories of others; those who have left us." Raine's eyes drifted away. "Their light—it can still remain." He quickly snapped back into focus. "But most importantly—we cannot escape memories. Even if they are suppressed, they are still there, somewhere. As such, we shouldn't think of them as simply things remembered, as they are with us all the time, and exist in so many shapes and forms. You see, I don't think it matters much when a memory occurred, but rather…" He stopped himself as he glanced away in thought before continuing. "It begs an intriguing question to be asked: At what point in time does a memory exist?"

Edyn sat quietly, deep in thought. It didn't dawn on him that Raine was asking a question that warranted a response.

Raine grabbed Edyn's attention, looking directly at him, and speaking with more conviction, "Can you answer that question, Edyn? Can any of us answer that question?" With even more emphasis this time, he repeated, "At what point in time does a memory exist?"

He actually wants me to answer this question?

"Well, it exists in the past."

"Does it?"

"Yeah, of course it does."

"I see. Hmm. But is it the past? What about the present? The future? Or what about all three?"

Okay, I'm pretty sure he's back to the rhetorical questions again.

"Sure, you are recalling a memory that indeed is from the past, but it is in the present when you experience it. You see, we exist in the present, but are also a part of our own or someone else's future memories of the past. How can this be? Whose memory are we in right now? And to be in someone's memory, someone would have to be thinking about us. How can that be? Maybe we need not question the point in time a memory exists, but rather, the point in time *we* exist?"

Raine stopped and gave another chuckle as he realized he had digressed much deeper than planned.

"Ah, apologies. Does any of that even matter? The memory is coming from somewhere—that is what is important. And the point I'm trying to make is that the timing itself is not so significant, nor is it something we can even fathom. Where a memory resides—*that* is the key, and that is what truly matters."

Edyn tried to process the flurry of context Raine had just thrown at him. He couldn't make sense of most of it.

"At what point in time does a memory exist?"

He finally mustered up a response. "I'm sorry. I guess I don't really understand what you're saying. I just wish I could know when my memory occurred. It's—"

"You weren't listening to what I was really asking," Raine interjected. "It doesn't matter at all the point in time the memory existed, if it could even be determined in the first place. Rather, where does the memory exist? Where does it reside? That is the true mystery, my friend." He nodded to himself reassuringly. "But there is a place. Those thoughts and memories that we have in our heads—they are somewhere."

Raine finished with confidence in his voice. "You see, Edyn, these are questions that cannot truly be answered. But what's important is to not single out a memory to try to deduce when it may have occurred. Rather, we must accept that all of our memories are a part of us, right now, and are existing somewhere.

6: COGNITION

All of yours are still a part of you, although it may be hard for you to accept this fact right now. But they are all still there, and they are in the same place they've always been, connected to you from that place, on a deeper level we do not yet fully understand. Wherever you are finding this clouded memory of the hill—this is the same place you'll find all the rest of the fleeting memories that have escaped you."

The point Raine was trying to make was finally getting through to Edyn. He nodded contentedly, his eyes showing a sense of both appreciation and determination.

"I know your memory the other night was an incredibly powerful experience for you, and I'm glad you opened up to me about it," Raine said, sitting up straightly in his chair. "I have something I want to try that I think might help you, but before we get to that, I do want to know: Was there anything else that happened to you the other night before or after your memory? Anything that didn't feel right to you or may have sparked it all?"

A terrible feeling came over Edyn as he recalled what he'd seen in the mirror just before passing out. He wanted to tell the doctor about the frightening image he'd seen but felt he wouldn't know how to describe it. But he knew his face was giving away the fact there was something he was hiding.

Quickly, he came up with a response. "Yeah, actually, there *was* something else that night. But it was later on, and I wouldn't really think anything of it."

Raine looked on with care as Edyn continued.

"Lately, I've been having this dream."

He told Raine all about his strange dream—about the black and empty expanse and the bright-blue beams of light streaking through it. He recounted the electrical sounds and being drawn to the glowing columned structure. He described its marbled pillars and the flowering vines growing around them. Lastly, he recalled the pedestal inside the structure, and the glowing object floating above it.

"Is that it?"

"Yeah, that's it." Edyn didn't mention the seemingly meaningless inscription on the pedestal nor the fact he'd heard that strange voice speak to him multiple times after the dream. "I wouldn't think too much of it. It's just a dream. But I've had it a couple of times now recently, and it feels a lot more real than a normal dream. But at the same time, it's just another illusion. Just like my recurring memory," he finished, sounding disheartened.

"Hmm. It is an odd dream, I will admit," Raine said. "But what dreams aren't odd? It sounds like a beautiful dream, and a beautiful setting, if you ask me." Feeling as though he needed to pick Edyn up, he added, "Now you know your recurring memory is more than just an illusion."

"I know…" Edyn replied.

"We know there is meaning behind it, and who knows, maybe there's meaning behind this dream too. Even if it is just an illusion to you now, illusions themselves are more real than you think. Just like illusions, you may only be interpreting part of it, which is making it seem as such."

In typical fashion, Raine saw this as an opportunity to relay more of his unique knowledge in an effort to help Edyn cope with and accept the nature of his condition.

"Every one of us sees illusions every day, you know." Raine searched his mind for the simplest example he could offer. "Take the sun and the sky above us. The sun is actually *white*. Our atmosphere separates the wavelengths of its light and scatters them across our sky. The shorter blue and violet wavelengths are more easily scattered, giving the sky its blue color. At the same time, it

6: COGNITION

changes our vision of the sun to yellow. As evening nears, more of the blue light is scattered as the sun's light travels further through the atmosphere from the horizon, giving us breathtaking sunsets with the remaining longer wavelengths of red, orange, and purple." He briefly glanced away, seemingly deep in thought. "That beautiful glow. The light that still remains." He returned his focus. "And even deeper still, the retinas of our eyes are what determines the light-blue daytime sky color we see, as opposed to its truer shade of violet-blue."

"Wow, I didn't know all of that," Edyn said, a look of amazement on his face.

"Exactly! And the sky is something you're surrounded by every single day! Something so common all throughout one's life, yet you could make the claim that it's nothing but an illusion." Raine continued excitedly. "Which leads us to the biggest illusion of all: time! This is an invisible concept that mankind created, and although it's a major part of all our daily lives, one could argue it does not exist. It is an illusion itself! It appears to be structured, but what exactly is it that we are structuring? The perception of time—this seems to change depending on what you're doing or thinking. And we even had the audacity to decide the flow of it! Simply one flat, linear direction—never deviating from that given path."

Knowing he'd already gotten his point across and was now going down a potential rabbit hole, Raine stopped himself, chuckling. "But that is another discussion for another time. We simply don't have the 'time' for it right now!"

Edyn offered a light laugh, but he was zoning out. His mind had been racing uncontrollably ever since Raine began sharing his thoughts on the concept of time.

Not getting the response he was hoping for, Raine tried to

summarize. "The point is that there is more to reality than what meets the eye. Illusions are all around us, so we can't so easily dismiss things as being 'just an illusion' as if they are any less real. What you see is what you see, and is just as real as the chair you are sitting in. If you think of it that way, you'll come to realize you're not seeing things any more hazily than the rest of us."

Raine was proud of the way he'd quickly tied all of that together, but soon his shoulders slumped and he let out a deep exhale. It seemed what he'd said hadn't gotten through to his patient at all. Edyn didn't respond or even acknowledge Raine's words.

Raine's mention of the flow of time and the world around him had sparked something deep within Edyn's mind. He didn't know exactly what, but there was some idea inside that was eluding him—something deep within the recesses of his mind that he simply could not bring to light.

He again caught himself transfixed by the piece of artwork on the wall in front of him: the white room with a spiral of colors approaching. The spiral appeared to move slowly toward him as it churned, as if projecting out of the artwork itself.

Edyn stared on, mesmerized as it crept closer and closer. He thought he might be able to reach out and touch it, and he extended his hand. At that moment, for only an instant, the room turned to black and the image was replaced by the bright-blue sideways spiral of energy he had seen in the mirror the other night.

I've created a connection.

A terrible fear crawled inside of Edyn and he jumped with a start, out of his seat. Raine popped up out of his chair. "What is it?

6: COGNITION

What did you see?!"

Edyn tried to gather himself. His heart was racing uncontrollably. He looked at Raine with distress in his eyes. "I... I don't know."

Raine put a hand on Edyn's shoulder. "It's okay. Everything is alright. I'm here for you." He guided Edyn to sit back down. "Please, take a few deep breaths."

Edyn followed Raine's orders, but it was no use, he couldn't calm himself.

Raine knew he needed to do something and immediately thought of an idea. There was a new therapy called Eye Movement Desensitization and Reprocessing, and he thought it might help.

"I would like for you to focus on my hand," Raine said, holding his right hand out, fingers held together. Edyn's disconcerted eyes locked onto Raine's hand. "I know you're still replaying in your head what you just experienced, and may be feeling negative thoughts. It's okay to have these thoughts, and I want you to hold on to them just a bit longer before letting go." Raine moved his hand back and forth from right to left. "Follow my hand with your eyes while still keeping these thoughts in mind."

Edyn followed Raine's instructions as the doctor continued. "The negative feelings you have are real, and you must accept them. Just keep watching my hand, and you'll see that these feelings are no more than just that, and they can be replaced. Please, continue to take deep breaths."

Edyn inhaled deeply and continued to watch Raine's hand but was still struggling to calm himself down.

"You don't need to hold on to these negative thoughts anymore," Raine said. "Watch my hand and recognize that you no longer need them."

Before long, he realized the therapy wasn't working. Edyn was still noticeably distressed. Raine began tapping his right foot on the floor in rhythm with the motion of his hand.

"Listen to the sounds. Release these thoughts, Edyn. Clear your mind."

Edyn fixated on the shoe-tapping and became overwhelmed with the fear of something approaching. He couldn't calm his racing mind and felt the room swirling around him.

The shoe-tapping sounds were then replaced by piercing electrical sounds that rang violently through his ears. He tried to shake them off, but they persisted, louder and louder.

Then, in an act of desperation, he covered his ears with his hands. But it was no use—the sounds only grew louder, cracking mercilessly in his ears. The room twisted and morphed around him.

Raine stood, a worried look on his face. Edyn thought he saw Raine try to say something, but he couldn't hear him. He was fading away.

Edyn then got lost within his mind, completely blacking out, with brief flashes of visions interrupting the darkness.

In one flash, Edyn saw a dying, desolate area with crumbled structures all around, and pillars of blue light beaming up to the sky above.

Another flash occurred, and he found himself inside a dark building, approaching an ominous-looking chamber, bright-blue light escaping through the cracks of its door.

A strong sense of familiarity overtook him, paired with a terrible fear that crept out from deep within.

Finally, a last vision manifested itself, and he approached a large, flashing image of the blue sideways spiral of energy. It flowed powerfully before him, its form and light pulsating with incredible force.

6: COGNITION

The fear within Edyn reached its apex as the strange voice again echoed within his head.

>――――――――/⁄――――――――
I know you can remember.
This is not reality.
>――――――――/⁄――――――――

7
RIFT

Later that night, Edyn tried to unwind on his couch, still struggling to make sense of what had happened and what he'd seen in Raine's office.

A knock at his door interrupted his still-racing thoughts. Edyn jumped up and just as another knock sounded, opened the door.

"Hi, Edyn." Serah, dressed only in thin gray sweatpants and a slim white T-shirt, stepped in and slipped off her shoes.

Wow...

Nerves overtook Edyn.

"Serah... you... don't you have work in the morning?" Edyn asked, stumbling over his words.

Seriously, why do I still get like this with her?

Serah wasn't her normal bubbly self. "Yeah. Sorry, I know it's late. It's just, I'm having a hard time winding down after what happened here the other night."

It dawned on Edyn that he didn't remember much else that had happened that night.

"I'm worried about you," Serah said. There was sadness in her eyes when she unexpectedly wrapped her arms around Edyn and rested her head against his chest. "That blank stare you had. It's like you weren't even there. I tried to snap you out of it, but I couldn't. It was scary for me to see you like that." She pulled back and looked into his eyes. "I had to help you to bed at the end of the night. Do you remember?"

Confused about the night's events, Edyn struggled to find the right words. "No... I... I don't know. I started seeing things and I don't remember much else after that. I must have blacked out or something. It's been happening to me."

"You know, I stayed by your side for a couple hours until I felt you were sleeping soundly."

Serah's eyes were heavy with worry as she looked at him. But there was something else in the way she was looking at him tonight.

"Listen, it's late," Edyn said. "I don't want to keep you up any longer worrying about me. I know there's been some weird things going on, but I'm gonna be okay. I promise. And I really have been making good progress with—"

Before he could finish his sentence, Serah quickly cried, "Edyn, I don't want to leave!" She embraced him tightly and buried her face in his chest. Edyn instinctively wrapped his arms around her.

Serah looked up longingly at him. "Do you think I could lay with you for a bit tonight? Just to make sure you fall asleep okay?"

Edyn felt a sudden jolt in his stomach. Her words were totally unexpected. Part of him was excited, but another part grew incredibly nervous. He hesitated briefly before replying, his words lacking conviction. "Yeah, sure. I mean, of course you can."

Smooth, Edyn.

Serah's eyes lit up and a smile broke across her face. "Thank you. It really would make me feel a lot better. And I promise I won't keep us up much longer. I know it's late. Let me freshen up real quick and we can get some shut-eye."

Edyn went to his bedroom while Serah went into the bathroom.

7: RIFT

His mind flew in all sorts of directions. This was all happening so fast, and he felt he needed time to mentally prepare. Scanning his room, he realized there was a lot he should straighten up before Serah came in, but there wasn't enough time.

Too late.

Moving quickly, he did the bare minimum—removing his socks, throwing on some shorts, reapplying his deodorant, straightening the bed cover. Finally, he sat down on his bed and listened as Serah finished up in the bathroom. Excitement began to overtake his nerves. But that excitement only masked the sharp pain in his head that had been slowly intensifying over the past few minutes.

I hope you understood my actions
All we have now is us
And you're all I need, but
I just couldn't go on living like this
It was inevitable
I had to try something
To see if we could have a future

I'm sorry, but
I have to leave you now
It's all my fault, so
Just don't think
There was anything you could have done
This is just how we have to end

We're going to be apart for a long time, but
If you get lost
Come back here
Just like we promised
I know you'll be able to find me

Keep me in your memories, Edyn
This is our goodbye
But I know I won't lose you forever, because
You'll still be where you've always been

Edyn came to surprisingly fast, moments before Serah entered the room. "What's wrong? You look like you've just seen a ghost," Serah said, continuing past Edyn to set some of her belongings on his dresser.

Catching Edyn completely off-guard, she removed her T-shirt, revealing only a slim black tank top. Edyn felt as if his heart skipped a beat when she turned to face him.

Serah smiled confidently and sat down on the bed beside him. "Look, Serah," Edyn said. "You know that memory of the hill I told you about that I have all the time?" Serah nodded. "Well, that's not the only thing about that memory. There's a woman in it, too. A woman I can't remember. She's speaking to me in it, and she's telling me... she's telling me goodbye."

Serah remained silent, seeming to struggle with what Edyn had just told her. "I'm sorry," she finally said. Then it seemed as if a few gears shifted in her head. "Wait a second. Was that why you were looking the way you were when I walked in? Did it just happen again?"

Edyn nodded. "Yeah. It's strange how often it happens, and

7: RIFT

how normal it's becoming for me. But still, I feel so terrible during it." He looked down. "And I can't even remember who she is."

A mixture of concern and disappointment was written on Serah's face. "I'm really sorry, Edyn. That must be so hard for you."

She paused, looking back and forth between Edyn's eyes as if she had something more she wanted to say, but her quivering lips remained silent. Then, gently, she put her hand on Edyn's back and stood. She walked back over to the dresser, removed her necklace, and carefully placed it next to her belongings.

"Now let's just try to get some good sleep. You've had quite the eventful past couple of days." She climbed into the far side of the bed and crawled under the covers.

So I guess that's her side.

Edyn flipped off the bedside lamp and got under the covers. He felt confused. He didn't quite know what to do or what Serah had expected, but she was immediately more distant since he'd told her more about the memory.

I shouldn't have told her that.

After a few moments, Serah broke the silence. "Edyn?"

"Yeah?"

"You know I'll be there for you if you need me. I just... I..." She seemed unsure about what she wanted to say. She then turned over to face away from him. "Goodnight, Edyn."

Edyn lay in the dark, confused by Serah's strange behavior. A few minutes passed before it dawned on him that he hadn't said goodnight back to her.

Sorry.

Disappointed in himself, Edyn turned over, shut his eyes, and drifted off. As he entered sleep, a few scattered dreams briefly appeared and faded before he found himself within the setting of a familiar one.

Once again, he walked slowly through the black expanse, guided by radiant blue streaks of light that led to a glowing hexagonal structure. The dream felt even more real to Edyn this time, and as he drifted closer to the white marbled columns, he could almost smell the flowers of the vines wrapped tightly around them. As he approached, electrical sounds intensified. Edyn saw something developing in the distance.

A thunderous boom cracked all around, and high in the black expanse beyond, a large fissure was ripping through. Bright white light shone through from the other side.

I am only trying to help you.

The entire scene trembled as Edyn stepped into the structure, the marbled columns surrounding him. He neared the white pedestal in the middle. Blue streaks of energy ran up its sides. The inscription atop it read *Ab Aeterno*.

A shining object floated above, as if presented by the pedestal. It was a collection of glowing golden lights in the shape of a symbol. Edyn looked closer and saw thirteen circles, six on the outside and seven on the inside, with lines from their centers connecting them to one another. In the distance, the fissure in the sky expanded farther. Edyn was drawn to the glowing object before him. He reached out to touch it.

7: RIFT

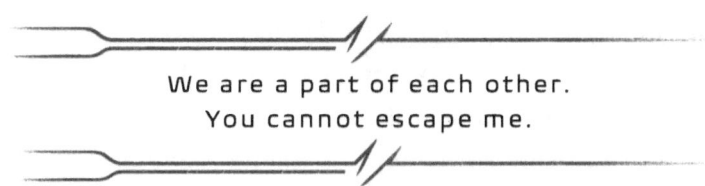

We are a part of each other.
You cannot escape me.

The moment his hand touched the object, Edyn was overtaken by a powerful energy. In an instant, the setting abruptly disappeared, replaced by another.

Where am I?

He was in a celestial setting, black space all around and stars above, standing on top of stone ruins. The pedestal stood before him, but he felt as if he'd just teleported someplace else. Someplace more than just a dream.

Edyn turned around. Before him rose large silver gates that stared ominously down at him. They seemed to lead nowhere; he saw only the nighttime sky beyond them. He moved closer for a better look and felt their incredible power as they towered high above.

The gates and the stone stiles connecting them stood at least twice as tall as Edyn and were covered in intertwined silver horns. The tops of the stiles were connected by patterns of steel, with the inviting gate doors underneath.

Edyn was drawn to the gates. As he approached, he extended his hands, grabbed onto the steel handles, and pulled. The gates creaked open and he stepped through.

Now he could see a short, winding path that extended out into the dark sky as if it were floating. At the end of the path was a glowing golden door. On either side of the glowing door appeared two statues in the shape of angels. Their faces were missing, a hole of nothingness taking their place.

He arrived at the door. It was beaming full of bright light, and patterns of golden horns covered it. He reached out to touch it but immediately pulled his hand away. It didn't feel as he'd expected. It felt like a wall of energy in the shape of a door, enticing him to step through.

Edyn took one last glance around him, drew a deep breath, and stepped into the glowing web of horns. With one step, he passed through the wall of energy to the other side. Oddly enough, he found himself in what looked like a mirror image of the gates he'd just stepped through. It was as if he were back where he'd started.

Confused, he walked toward the gates ahead, but once through them, quickly realized this was not the same place at all. There was a wide, rocky path before him with an abyss on either side. The air was cold, and a misty fog curled throughout the darkness ahead. His determination and curiosity were gone. Edyn felt he was in a place he shouldn't be.

He turned to go back but stopped in his tracks. He saw that there was something different about the gates on this side.

Although the structure of the gates appeared the same as before, the patterns covering them were different. Instead of silver horns, rows of ivory covered their entire mass.

Eager to get out of this place, Edyn passed back through the gates and down the short path that led to the glowing door. As he neared, he saw that this door, too, looked slightly different on this side.

Without hesitation, he walked through the wall of energy before him, but instead of stepping through webs of golden horns, he walked through patterns of light ivory.

Once on the other side, Edyn darted back to the pedestal and touched the glowing symbol hovering above it. In an instant, he was back inside the columned structure. The surroundings had completely deteriorated, torn apart by the ever-increasing fissure.

7: RIFT

The blinding light was intensifying. The dream was fading.

Before he knew it, everything around him vanished, engulfed by the light, and Edyn escaped to a dark and empty place deep within the stray corridors of his mind.

8
COALESCENCE

Edyn was surrounded by black emptiness, lost within the depths his subconscious. His mind began to run wild, filling the void with haunting visions that appeared before him.

He found himself back at the dying, desolate area he'd seen in brief flashes while in Raine's office. Only this time, he felt as if he were actually there. He could feel the scorching heat of the sun as he scanned the abandoned place in ruins, and he saw bright-blue pillars of light coming from its crumbled structures, beaming up high into the sky above.

Next, he was deep inside a dark building, walking down a long set of metal stairs that led to an ominous chamber, blue light escaping through the cracks of its door. Feelings of loneliness and lost hope took hold of him. As he walked, his footsteps echoing, he could have sworn he heard other footsteps and faint yells. It was as if he were surrounded by ghosts.

No sooner had he entered the chamber than he felt a familiar fear. Rising before him was a blue sideways spiral of energy. It flowed powerfully on the other side of a glass-like surface. The blue energy was curling and pulsing, illuminating the chamber with its blinding glow, and vibrating it with its deafening low-pitched hums.

Advanced computers and electrical equipment filled out the rest of the chamber. Beyond the blinding light and advanced machinery was the blurry image of a man. The man appeared to be connected to the machinery. Edyn couldn't tell who he was or what he was trying to do. He sat motionless, his back to Edyn, his right hand reaching out to his right. Edyn followed where the hand was pointing and saw a door at the far end of the room.

Curious, Edyn made his way to the door and, without hesitation, opened it. On the other side was a dark and empty room, filled only with a large bright screen on the far wall. On the screen, a familiar scene was being projected. Edyn approached the haunting image shown before him.

What is this?

Confusion and terror rained down on Edyn as an image of the hill from his recurring memory was displayed on the screen. But this time, the grass and vegetation were missing, and the setting was in a desolate state. He moved closer for a better look, but the screen abruptly went blank, and the room was plunged into darkness.

Behind him, in the doorway, a man he couldn't see spoke with a familiar voice. "You... How? How are you here right now?"

Before Edyn could react, everything vanished and he found himself back in a dark and empty state, lost within his own mind.

Overcome with fear, Edyn frantically searched through the dark void for any sign of light. Finally, he caught something out of the corner of his eye. He turned and saw sparkling purple leaves falling through the darkness. He followed them as more and more appeared, lighting the way forward.

8: COALESCENCE

Eventually the darkness subsided, and a path appeared before him. He followed it until it generated into a winding trail up a grassy hill, and Edyn began the climb. Advancing through waves of tall grass, he heard the surf crashing into the rocks on the other side of the hill, and he could almost smell the water.

Ascending the hill, he saw the figure of a woman facing away from him. As he drew closer, he saw that she was gazing up at the gigantic moon overhead. It shone brightly, illuminating the nighttime setting with its radiant glow.

At the top of the hill, Edyn sat beside the standing woman and for the first time could see her clearly. Her petite figure was clothed in a black dress, and long black hair flowed down past her bare shoulders. A flurry of emotions washed over him when she turned to him with her soft, angelic face. She wore a distant smile, but sadness was shining through.

She turned her gaze downward to the rocks below for a moment before sitting down beside him and turning to him with her piercing blue-green eyes.

Edyn recognized her. But he didn't know how.

Her lips moved, but all he could initially hear were the muffled sounds of her familiar voice. Gradually, it became audible.

What happens next
It doesn't matter
I love you, Edyn

I hope you understood my actions
All we have now is us
And you're all I need, but
I just couldn't go on living like this

AFTERGLOW

It was inevitable
I had to try something
To see if we could have a future

I'm sorry, but
I have to leave you now
It's all my fault, so
Just don't think
There was anything you could have done
This is just how we have to end

We're going to be apart for a long time, but
If you get lost
Come back here
Just like we promised
I know you'll be able to find me

Keep me in your memories, Edyn
This is our goodbye
But I know I won't lose you forever, because
You'll still be where you've always been

Edyn woke with a start, his mind racing.

"*You'll still be where you've always been…*"

He recalled these words, over and over. They felt as if they were unlocking his mind. He knew there was something important about them.

Who are you?

9
PARALLELS

"I think he's waking up! Edyn! Edyn!"

Edyn slowly opened his eyes and gained awareness while the image of the woman in his head was replaced by another.

"You're awake!" Serah sat beside him, tears of joy welling in her eyes.

Edyn found himself on a hospital bed. "Serah, where are we?"

"At the Riverwood Hospital," she said. "Edyn, you never woke up this morning. Or, I guess I should say, I couldn't wake you up."

"What?"

"At first I thought you just needed more sleep, but I didn't want to leave you, so I called off work and let you sleep the rest of the morning. But later, after I still couldn't wake you up, I knew something must be wrong. So I called an ambulance around one o'clock. You've been here all day."

"Really?" Edyn seemed skeptical of the whole situation. "What time is it?"

Serah glanced at her wrist. "Almost 7:00 p.m."

Edyn was shocked to hear how much time had passed. "Wow. Listen, Serah, I'm sorry."

"Don't apologize! I'm just glad you're okay. I was so worried about you." She placed her hand on Edyn's and squeezed tightly. "You know, for a short time, I could have sworn you weren't in your room. One time when I checked on you, you weren't there, so I went looking around your apartment and out in the hallway. But by the time I came back in and peeked inside your room, you were there again. Strange, I know. Maybe I was just freaking out so much that I imagined it? Or maybe you were sleepwalking?"

"Yeah, maybe," Edyn replied without giving too much attention.

Although he was awake and fully aware, his head was still foggy, and even the room had a certain haze to it.

Where was I?

A nurse walked past the open door, saw the two talking to each other, and came in. "Ah, you're awake! How are you feeling, Edyn?"

"Uh, okay," he replied groggily.

"Good, good," the nurse said. "Now you just relax there with your friend and I'll go notify the doctors."

Edyn turned back to Serah. "*Am* I okay? Did they say anything to you about me?"

"Well, from what I heard, they weren't too sure. After a few tests and scans, they told me it didn't seem like anything was wrong. But I'll admit, they didn't seem too sure about anything." Then, with a touch of sarcasm, she added, "Great diagnosis, I know. But I guess all of that is good news."

Edyn exhaled. He noticed Serah was still holding his hand tightly. "Thanks so much for everything. For taking care of me, you know."

"Of course," she said, looking intently at him. "I couldn't leave you like that. And listen, I'm sorry about last night. I know it may have seemed like I was acting weird, and just how everything was

9: PARALLELS

so abrupt and all. I know it might have been confusing to you. It's just—"

Before she could continue, the nurse popped back in. Edyn felt a sharp pain in his head, and his vision flickered. The nurse promptly unhooked the cords of a few monitoring devices from Edyn's head and chest and adjusted his bed to a more upright position. "Well," she said, "I have good news for you. You're not required to stay here much longer. The doctors didn't find anything abnormal, and you'll be released shortly."

She set Edyn's stack of clothing next to him. He pulled himself upright, but before he could reply, the nurse, who seemed to be in a rush, headed for the door.

"Take your time," she called behind her. "But when you're ready, make sure you stop by the desk down the hall before you leave. There are just a few questions and clarification items we need from you about some of your personal info."

Edyn gave a sigh.

I hate having to answer to these things.

He moved to get out of the bed and saw how happy Serah looked. He waited a moment for what he thought would happen, but it didn't. Hesitantly, he said, "So I guess I'll just get dressed real quick, and then we can—"

Before he could finish, Serah, realizing her error, interjected, "Oh! Sorry! I'll step out for a moment!"

While Edyn put his clothes back on, he took another look around the room, still curious about how he'd ended up here.

What is going on with me?

When he was dressed, he left the room to find Serah waiting patiently outside the door. He looked past her and down the hallway. He saw a desk and two men dressed in dark corporate attire with briefcases in hand, talking to a doctor. One of the men looked in Edyn's direction. He began to feel uneasy.

Serah had a smirk on her face. It was the side of Serah he knew well but hadn't seen much of since the museum party. She broke the silence. "Hey, so do you wanna just get out of here?" She took a glance down the other end of the hallway. "I mean, we can definitely exit a different way, and I don't think you're required to stay any longer or anything."

Edyn weighed his options, but Serah continued. "It's just, there's only about an hour of sunlight left, and there's this really nice park nearby that we could visit before sundown. Whaddaya say?"

Edyn smiled and simply nodded, confirming the plan, and the two initiated their sneaky escape.

Only a few blocks away, Edyn and Serah arrived at the park and walked through a field of grass toward the middle. There was a small stream in view ahead, which could faintly be heard, and vibrant colored flowers were scattered all around.

As they walked, Serah shot quick glances at Edyn before turning to look back ahead. He noticed but didn't think anything of it.

Whether it was the sounds of nature or just being out of the hospital, Edyn felt very much at peace in this moment. The setting felt dreamlike with its beauty and tranquility. It reminded him of a place he used to visit in his past.

"It's beautiful here, isn't it?" Serah said. Sparkling water flowed gently over rocks, birds chirped all around, and the sun was setting on the open field in the distance.

"It really is," Edyn said.

Serah took a few steps away from Edyn toward the edge of the stream. She appeared to be toying with something around her neck as she gazed at the setting sun. Still facing away from him, she

9: PARALLELS

asked, "Do you think certain people were meant to cross paths?"

Edyn, caught completely off-guard by such a serious question, didn't know what to say. "Um, I don't know. I mean, yeah. Sure."

Serah spun around to face him. "You know, I feel like I've known you longer than I have." Her eyes were heavy with tenderness. "Or even like I've *always* known you. I don't know what it is, but I've always felt that way with you. Just so comfortable, right from the moment we bumped into each other in the hallway. But I worry about you, Edyn, and I want to take care of you when you need it. I just wish I could." She paused and looked down. "I just want what's best for you."

"You know," Edyn said, "I've felt the same way. I can't tell you enough how grateful I am to have someone like you—"

But before he could say any more, Serah interjected, "But you don't feel the same way!" She exhaled, trying to calm herself. "Sorry. I mean, not exactly the same way. It's just… there's things inside telling me all that we're never going to be."

"What do you mean?"

She looked all around as if searching for the right words to say, her torn feelings visible. "You're right in front of me, Edyn, but it's like I can't find you. You're somewhere else. The woman you can't remember—you must be so connected to her." She swallowed and her voice trembled when she spoke again. "You must have really loved her. And I want to help you. So that you'll eventually remember. And find her."

Serah looked to the ground, and Edyn took her by her hands. "Serah, I'm sorry. I'm so sorry. I do really care about you. There's just so much with me that's confusing, and we still don't even really know who that woman was to me."

"Stop it!" she snapped. "You must know, deep down, someplace. You have to know what she must have been to you, right? And how you still feel for her?" Her sadness dissipated and she continued, her voice more assured. "It's okay, I've accepted all of this. But it doesn't mean that I still can't be *something* to you. I want to be close with you, and I know I still can be, in a way. I'm going to do my best. I really care about you, above all else."

"Serah..." Edyn moved in to embrace her, but he quickly pulled away. A sharp pain shot through his head, and he put his hand up to it to brace himself as piercing sounds rang through his ears.

"What's wrong? Are you okay?"

This time, the pain faded more quickly than usual. "Yeah, just a little headache, that's all."

"Here," Serah said, motioning toward a nearby bench. "Let's take a seat."

They sat side by side, listening to the sound of the water and enjoying the view as the horizon was bathed in the golden glow of the setting sun.

Edyn looked at Serah, who seemed deep in thought, again toying with her necklace. Edyn looked closer and saw her fingers working around a charm at the end of it. Suddenly, a strange feeling came over him, and he felt a jolt inside. The charm was familiar.

It bore a symbol created by a collection of small circles—a ring of six on the outside with more packed within—all woven together by lines connecting their centers. He knew he'd seen something like it before but couldn't remember what.

Serah turned to look at him and her face, along with their surroundings, flickered. Seeing Edyn staring at her charm, she said, "This was my mother's. My father gave it to me just before he passed." She gripped it tightly. "It's pretty, huh?"

"Yeah, it is."

"It's actually a symbol that shows up from time to time in the ancient art we have on display at the museum," she said. "It's a

9: PARALLELS

form of what we refer to as 'sacred geometry.' This one has a really deep meaning."

Something clicked in Edyn's mind and he instinctively spoke, "Metatron's Cube."

"How did you know that?" Serah asked, shocked.

He thought hard but truly didn't know how he knew the name. "I'm not really sure. Lucky guess, I suppose."

How did I know that?

"Yeah, I'll say," Serah said. "Anyways, it's something that I keep with me. My connection with my mother, you know, since I never met her—it's not so different from yours with the woman you can't remember. But I do have such strong feelings for her, and it helps me when I'm feeling down."

Her voice took on a hint of sadness again. "I know I seem cheerful most of the time, but the truth is, sometimes I'm acting like that to cover up what I'm really feeling inside. There's been things that have happened to me in my past that left me in a dark place, and feeling dark things. And sometimes, those feelings come back." She looked longingly at Edyn. "But I don't feel that way when I'm with you."

Edyn wanted to say something but couldn't quite find the words.

"Your light, Edyn—it brings me out of the dark." She seemed to drift off for a moment. "I know things are going good for me. It's just, there *was* someone..." A knot formed in her throat, and her eyes welled up with tears. "They say if someone leaves you and they come back, you should love them forever." She sniffed and wiped away a stray tear falling from her eye. "But they don't tell you what to do if they leave you again."

Edyn put his arm around her. "Serah..."

"It's okay. Really. I know I can't get those years back, but I've finally let it go. I've let *him* go. And I know now that his feelings weren't true. They never were. They were just... they were just naked lies." She looked up and gazed at the sunset in the distance. "And with others, well..." She turned back to Edyn. "Do you ever think you would have been perfect for someone in another life? You know, things didn't quite line up or work out in this one, but in another one, you just know that they would?"

Edyn thought hard on it and conveyed his feelings by offering her his hand.

Gripping his hand, Serah spoke again, her voice holding a trace of hope. "But you know, I'm glad I'm not living any of those other lives."

"Why not?" Edyn asked as the two gazed at the sparkling stream, the light of the setting sun reflecting off it.

Serah moved closer to Edyn and rested her head on his shoulder. She felt the sadness inside of her transforming into a different emotion as warmness filled her heart. "Because I'm here with you, right now, in this one."

10
AB AETERNO

"I'm so sorry, Edyn. They should have sent for me while you were there. I would have come by immediately."

Raine was pacing around his office, trying to piece together everything Edyn told him had happened yesterday, and about how he'd wound up at the hospital. He recounted to Raine the same version of the story Serah had told him, and for the past couple of minutes, Raine had been deliberating on how and why it could have happened.

Edyn was less concerned about what caused his state of unconsciousness than he was about what happened during it, and what he'd seen when he experienced the memory. Still in a mild state of shock, he stared down into his lap and spoke with a quivering voice. "I saw her."

Raine didn't appear to hear Edyn. He continued pacing, seemingly lost in his thoughts.

"Raine," Edyn implored again, with more determination in his voice. "I *saw* her. The woman from my memory."

This time, Raine stopped dead in his tracks and spun around to face Edyn, adjusting his glasses. "You *what?*"

Edyn nodded assuredly. "I did. I was actually able to see her this time. Vividly."

Raine pulled up his chair and sat beside Edyn, eager to learn more. "This is truly amazing. The progress that is happening…" He fumbled feverously through his notes. "Can you please explain all that you saw?"

This was the most excitement Edyn had seen from Raine since their sessions began. And while he knew Raine was asking about the woman, he couldn't help but think about everything else he'd seen and experienced during the eerie period of time before awakening at the hospital. He was still confused and horrified by the things he'd witnessed, unsure if they were visions, memories, or dreams.

The desolate area, the chamber, the blue spiral of energy, the man who spoke to him, and the projection on the screen. None of it made any sense, and his recollection of them was clouded. But he did clearly remember the recurring memory he'd experienced just before waking—this time being able to vividly see the woman speaking to him.

Edyn described everything he'd seen and experienced, down to the last detail. When he was finished, told Raine, "I recognized her. I just can't figure out how."

"This is such great news!" Raine exclaimed excitedly. "You are really starting to remember! We are making such great progress, and quickly!" He clasped his hands together and leaned forward, eyes intent. "Now, in this latest rendition of your memory, is there anything else she is saying to you that is different than before?"

Edyn thought for a moment. "Yes. The furthest back I can remember now, she tells me that she loves me. After that, it's just what I've told you before. Her talking about how she's leaving me, and saying goodbye."

"This is it," Raine declared, as if something he'd been

considering was now validated. "The trauma. I am deducing that it is indeed from this love that was lost. I know you have been confused about who exactly this woman was to you. But it is clear now, this had to have been your past lover, and losing her must have been what triggered the onset of your psychogenic amnesia."

"I know we've speculated that was a strong possibility," Edyn countered, "but there must be more to it than that, right? I'm realizing now who she was to me, especially after what I felt when I saw her face. But something tells me there has to be more to this than just the fact that I lost her. Right?"

Raine nodded his head in agreement. "Yes, yes. But of course. With all that you've told me, and all of the other unusual events you've been experiencing, I agree there is still much more to this puzzle to decipher. I speculate that losing this woman was the climax and culmination of events that led to your condition, however, we still aren't exactly sure what the circumstances were. We still need to figure out what happened beforehand, prior to this goodbye. But I am certain that something about this particular event or point in time is what traumatized you."

Edyn tried to feel content about the progress that had been made, and although what Raine was saying made a great deal of sense to him, he was still grappling with mixed emotions.

Raine continued. "Remember, this is your therapy. There isn't anything physical about your condition. It's all about treating your mind and unlocking it even more. We know we can because we already have." He glanced down at his notes. "There's one more critical piece that I think would unlock so much more, if only you could remember it."

"What's that?"

"Isn't it obvious?" Raine replied. "Her name, of course."

Edyn nodded. That was still a big mystery.

I don't have any idea what it is.

"If you can think deeply and try to truly accept this event that caused your condition, I believe you could remember her name," Raine said. "And if that happens, I believe we would be able to unlock so much more."

He took the opportunity to shift gears.

"Now, I want us to try something. Please sit back and relax in your chair."

Edyn leaned back in the chaise lounge and tried to get himself as comfortable as possible.

"I want you to picture the scene," Raine continued. "Your memory, that is. Close your eyes and try to recreate the image in your mind."

Edyn nodded, closed his eyes, and sank into the memory. He imagined himself walking up the hill, trying his best to envision the entire setting in full.

"Now, I want you to take a step back from it all and really try to take in this place, almost from a bird's-eye viewpoint. Who is there?"

Edyn viewed it all from high above. He pictured himself reaching the top of the hill.

"Who are you looking at?" Raine asked.

Edyn focused down on himself atop the hill, next to the woman in the black dress.

"Yes... look even closer," Raine coaxed.

The more he concentrated, the more Edyn felt uneasy, as intense feelings of sadness grew inside of him. The scene in his head began to swirl.

"Who is the woman you are looking at?" Raine asked. "And more importantly, who is the 'you'?"

Edyn was suddenly overwhelmed, feeling as though he

10: AB AETERNO

transported directly into the memory itself, and he vividly re-experienced it.

It'll be like we never knew each other
It wasn't supposed to end like this
What happens next
It doesn't matter
I love you, Edyn

I hope you understood my actions
All we have now is us
And you're all I need, but
I just couldn't go on living like this
It was inevitable
I had to try something
To see if we could have a future

I'm sorry, but
I have to leave you now
It's all my fault, so
Just don't think
There was anything you could have done
This is just how we have to end

We're going to be apart for a long time, but
If you get lost
Come back here
Just like we promised
I know you'll be able to find me

> Keep me in your memories, Edyn
> This is our goodbye
> But I know I won't lose you forever, because
> You'll still be where you've always been

Piercing electrical noises rang, and the terrifying sound of the other strange voice echoed within Edyn's head.

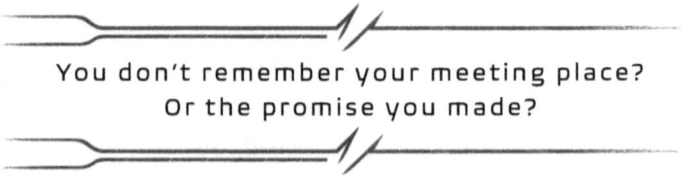

> **You don't remember your meeting place?
> Or the promise you made?**

Stricken with fear, Edyn felt paralyzed, his mouth gaping open.

"Meeting place?"

"Promise?"

Who are you?

Raine was there at his side, trying to shake him out of it. "Edyn! Edyn! Are you alright? Did it happen again? Did you see her?"

Deflecting from his fear and hiding what he had just heard from Raine, Edyn answered, "Yeah, it did. I saw her again, but still, not much else. I still can't remember anything about her. Let alone her name." He shook his head, his voice reflecting a sense of lost hope. "I just can't take this anymore, Raine. How is it I can be so deeply connected to a woman I can't remember?"

Raine put a comforting hand on Edyn's back to reassure him. "Remember, Edyn, you do remember who she is. It's just that your mind has decided to suppress it. But you are still very much connected to her, and her memory."

10: AB AETERNO

Raine returned to his seat, debating whether he should share an applicable concept he'd studied frequently that might help his patient understand. Meanwhile, Edyn gazed straight ahead, a hopeless expression on his face.

"I know we've discussed this before," Raine began, "but there is just so much about our minds that we simply do not understand. Our mental and emotional capacities—they work in such mysterious ways. You are deeply connected to this woman, but in ways you cannot tell, see, or measure. You may not think you remember her, but really, your mind does remember. And it will always remember, somewhere."

Raine adjusted the collar of his shirt, as if preparing himself before sharing the details of the concept.

"There are some that argue we're all connected in this way, in an 'atmosphere of the minds.' They have a name for this philosophical concept: the noosphere. I've done quite a bit of research on it myself and, in summary, the claim is that we all contribute to this living, growing, grand sphere of human thought and consciousness enveloping the Earth. The psyche of all humans, connected to one another. The natural evolution of the Earth where our collective consciousness and intelligence builds upon and reshapes the geosphere and biosphere."

Raine continued. "I will admit, it is quite speculative. And the technology to be able to measure such things, indeed, may never exist. But I must say, with all that I've learned throughout my years, I do believe something along these lines truly does exist. I think it is highly likely there is at least some type of radial or spiritual energy that we simply cannot measure. Now, you can see that certainly if anything in this regard were true, then you would be especially connected with this woman, and that connection will always remain. Her light, Edyn, it still shines within you."

Edyn wasn't taking in much of what Raine was saying. Instead, he was transfixed by the sunlight streaming in through the windows spanning the top of the wall before him. The glow mesmerized him, and he tried to follow the ray's path into the room. It made him think back on the dream, the way the light radiated from the pedestal within the columned structure, and the bright glowing object hovering above it.

A jolt of fear shot through him when he recalled what happened the last time he experienced the dream—passing through the gates and ending up in a dark place that terrified him. The fear snapped him out of his trance, and he abruptly stood. "Raine, I think I need to get out of here. My head—I just can't get it to settle." He stumbled a moment, searching for words. "I just need to get my mind off all of this for a little while. Can we take a break?"

"Of course, Edyn!" Raine said. "This has been quite an eventful past few days for you. I think a short break from all of this is a great idea." Raine paused, seemingly holding something back. "You know, I'm so proud of you, Edyn. None of this is easy, and in a case such as yours, well… I know you might not think so yourself, but you truly are handling it with such grace and strength."

In that moment, it struck Edyn just how much Raine genuinely cared for him. He felt more than just a patient. He felt like a friend.

Edyn smiled appreciatively. "Thanks. All of that is probably because I've had such a great teacher."

Raine smiled contentedly as he watched Edyn move toward his office door. "Goodbye, Edyn. Give yourself as much time as you need and get back to me whenever you're ready."

But Edyn stopped, fixated on something else from the dream that never quite made sense to him. The inscription atop the pedestal had been in some foreign language. He'd almost forgotten

10: AB AETERNO

about it. He turned back to Raine. "Sorry, just one more thing. Do you know what 'Ab Aeterno' means?"

Raine gave Edyn a perplexed look, confused by why he'd ask such a random question, but swiftly answered, "Of course! I know more than enough Latin to know *that* translation. Eight-plus years of psychology schooling will do that for you!" He chuckled to himself. "It means something that is from an infinitely remote time in the past. It could even mean something that is from a place existing outside of time itself. 'From the eternal,' 'from the everlasting,' or, quite simply, 'from infinity.' "

11
ILLUSIA

"*From infinity?*"
It was the middle of the afternoon. The cries of seagulls and gently crashing waves filled the air. Edyn was walking down the sidewalk on his way home, still pondering Raine's translation. Something about that last line stuck hard. What was it about that strange inscription?

He was only a block from Raine's office, near the boardwalk, when his vision again flickered. But this time was different—it wasn't going away. The flickering intensified in strength and duration, and piercing electrical sounds rang loudly in his ears. He spun around and saw the entirety of his surroundings were being affected too.

Panic set in, and he moved quickly toward the boardwalk. His vision grew increasingly distorted. He saw the faces of those he walked past giving him strange looks.

Then, abruptly, it all ceased.

Edyn found himself standing at the edge of the boardwalk. But the daytime setting was replaced with the black of the night. All was quiet. He looked out at the ominous, still water of the ocean. Moonlight shone down from above and reflected onto it. The town behind him had fallen completely silent. The boardwalk itself was empty and dark, with only a few stray flickering streetlights.

But the silence lasted only briefly. The flickering returned, rapidly increasing in strength until it became so intense that Edyn shielded his eyes, lost in confusion.

Finally, it ceased. Gathering courage, Edyn slowly reopened his eyes. What he saw next left him in utter disbelief. He was back in the mysterious setting from his dream.

Edyn moved forward through the black expanse, guided by the radiant blue streaks of light that led to the glowing hexagonal structure ahead. Again, his movement felt controlled as he was pulled along. Sparking electrical sounds rang, rising in volume and intensity the closer he came to the glowing marble structure.

Flowering vines wrapped around the white columns, and Edyn inhaled their scent as a thunderous crack sounded. An immense fissure began to rip through the black sky in the distance.

Everything began trembling violently as he put his hand on one of the marbled columns and stepped up and into the structure. The fissure in the sky was widening, and a blinding white light was escaping through from the other side. The ground below him shook as small rocks crumbled from the structure's top.

He approached the pedestal before him. Bright-blue streaks of energy ran up its sides.

He read the inscription at the top: *Ab Aeterno.*

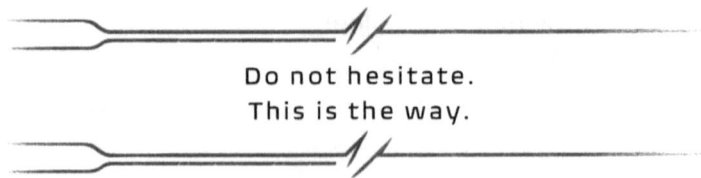

Do not hesitate.
This is the way.

11: ILLUSIA

Above the pedestal, a floating symbol made of glowing golden lights presented itself. Its thirteen circles—six on the outside and seven on the inside, with lines connecting their centers—emitted light from all angles.

Instinctively, Edyn reached out and touched it, while his surroundings rapidly deteriorated. At once, he was overcome by a powerful energy, and was taken to another place.

As before, Edyn was standing atop stone ruins within a celestial setting, nothing but black space and emptiness surrounding. Knowing what he would see, he turned and once again set his eyes upon the large silver gates rising ominously before him. Edyn advanced to the gates, their power weighing on him as they towered high above.

With more confidence than he'd had the last time, Edyn grabbed the gate handles and pulled. The heavy doors, covered in intertwined silver horns, creaked open just enough for him to step through. He saw the winding path ahead. It extended out into the dark sky as if it were floating, and there was a beaming golden door at the end of it, just as before.

As he walked the path, he again saw frightening statues of angels with their faces missing at the foot of either side of the glowing door. Edyn recalled what he'd seen and experienced the last time he'd stepped through it, and how quickly he'd turned back, but this time something inside was telling him to continue onward. He took one last deep breath and entered the wall of energy, stepping through its web of golden horns.

Just as before, when he emerged on the other side he saw a mirror of the gates he'd just stepped through. He approached the silver gates ahead and confidently passed through them. He closed the gate doors behind him and again noticed the difference in their patterns on this side. Both the gates and the small door of glowing light were covered in rows of ivory, light and opaque.

He regarded his eerie new surroundings. A wide rocky path lay ahead, barely visible through a cold and misty fog, and an abyss bordered either side of it. Frightening sounds echoed in the distance, and shadows shifted in the air.

Edyn marched forward, but before he went too far, loud creaking sounds came from behind. He quickly turned around. The gates were closing and were being engulfed by the thick fog, disappearing from sight. Edyn ran back toward them in desperation as they continued to fade.

No!

But by the time he reached them, the gates had vanished, replaced only by the curling fog. Edyn stumbled backward in fear.

His foot caught on to something and he fell hard to the ground, landing mere feet from the edge of the path and the abyss beyond. He quickly moved his body to the center of the path and set his gaze down the way forward, away from where the gates had stood.

A small bright light was shifting its way through the air toward him. He squinted, trying to make out what it was. It flew straight at him and he ducked as it zipped over his head. When he picked his head back up, he saw the light stop where the gates had been and start to race back in his direction.

What is this?

This time, it stopped a few feet away from him. To Edyn's shock, it spoke. "What are you doing down there?"

Edyn picked himself up. "Who... *what*... are you?"

The tiny figure appearing to be a sprite, with a light almost too blinding to see, answered in a high-pitched voice. "Me? I am Echo. Something from the past that doesn't exist anymore, but yet does. Then again, there is no past anymore."

With that, he sped away, and Edyn thought he heard a laugh.

11: ILLUSIA

What?

Edyn watched as Echo raced back down the path and momentarily disappeared. But he returned in a matter of seconds, coming back into focus as he again sped directly toward Edyn. "This place can be different for everyone. It is everything, and anything, and the *only* thing."

He zigged and zagged in the air, seemingly unable to hold still. Edyn studied him cautiously, not knowing what to say.

Echo spoke again. "You are special." He zipped behind Edyn. "But you are not so different from me." He zipped back in front of Edyn again. "You are something that used to be, that is not yet to be, yet is here with me."

Echo again sped away down the path as Edyn desperately shouted after him, "Wait! What are you talking about?!"

In the distance, Edyn heard Echo's fading words as his light dissipated. "Seek the Forgotten, the Three. They can provide the answers, you see." His glow dimmed until it disappeared entirely.

Edyn waited, fully expecting Echo to return, but it didn't happen. Shaking off the baffling encounter, Edyn's eyes followed the path before him as far as they would allow. He took a determined step forward and began his journey.

The air was cold, and Edyn tried to make out what lay within the misty fog ahead as he ventured through the darkness.

Where am I?

Soon, Edyn began to see bright and colorful lights ahead, sparking his hope. He picked up his pace, eager to see what awaited him. With each step, the lights intensified.

Vividly colored vegetation sprouted from all around him, as if a forest was manifesting itself through the darkness. The greenery spread with each step he took, until the abyss was no more and Edyn was instead surrounded by illuminated scenery.

The forest was colorful and dense. Purple and blue lights shone from the tops of the vegetation, glowing through the darkness. He traversed the forest, stepping over grass and flowers underfoot while the sounds of unseen animals and insects filled the air.

But to Edyn's despair, his newfound surroundings abruptly changed, retreating just as rapidly as they had come. This continued until Edyn found himself alone in a dry wasteland.

He looked down helplessly to the hot cracks in the ground below. At once, the cracks filled with water coming from underground. The water level increased, eventually covering Edyn's ankles. As it intensified, a sense of hopelessness washed over him, while a shallow sea took shape around him. Edyn breathed a sigh of relief when the rising sea stopped at his waist.

Surrounding him was an open sea with a blue tree standing in the middle straight ahead. Everything was illuminated by moonlight.

What is this place?

Am I really here right now?

He walked through the water, slowly splashing his way toward the mysterious tree. As he drew closer, he noticed something peculiar about it: Deep-blue water fell from its branches, filling up the sea and giving the tree its blue color.

He cupped his hands beneath the falling water, letting them fill up, and drank. As soon as he did, he noticed that the water falling into his hands was slowing. It continued to slow until it suddenly began racing back up the tree in reverse.

Edyn braced himself as a rush of waves crashed into him as the water rapidly traveled back up the tree. He closed his eyes and held on. Finally, it subsided and the waves were no more. He opened his eyes. The tree and water were gone, replaced by the dark, misty void.

11: ILLUSIA

The next few minutes played tricks on Edyn's fragile mind. As he pressed on, fleeting visions and memories from his youth played out before his very eyes. But every time he tried to get closer to them, they vanished. The images were right in front of him, but remained far out of reach.

Eventually, he broke and fell to his knees. He didn't know what any of the memories meant, or where he was, but he didn't have time to dwell. A magnificent sight began to take shape in front of him. The wind swirled, and the images of the scattered memories morphed together to produce the image of a single one. The hill loomed ahead.

Before he could stand up to approach it, he was instantly taken there. He was sitting next to the beautiful woman in black. She stood gazing up at the moon hanging overhead, her form again fully vivid. She smiled when she looked over at him, but her face showed sadness. She peered down at the rocks below for a moment and sat down beside him.

Powerful emotions rushed through Edyn as he viewed the despair upon the woman's face. This time, when she spoke her first words, she was fighting against the tears that fell from her turquoise eyes.

And this might be our only option
We have to try

It'll be like we never knew each other
It wasn't supposed to end like this
What happens next

AFTERGLOW

It doesn't matter
I love you, Edyn

I hope you understood my actions
All we have now is us
And you're all I need, but
I just couldn't go on living like this
It was inevitable
I had to try something
To see if we could have a future

I'm sorry, but
I have to leave you now
It's all my fault, so
Just don't think
There was anything you could have done
This is just how we have to end

We're going to be apart for a long time, but
If you get lost
Come back here
Just like we promised
I know you'll be able to find me

Keep me in your memories, Edyn
This is our goodbye
But I know I won't lose you forever, because
You'll still be where you've always been

11: ILLUSIA

The memory vanished. Edyn, still on his knees, found himself back within a dark and cloudy place.

"You'll still be where you've always been."

Hearing her say those words through her tears was agonizing, but there was something familiar about them. Before he could dwell for too long, he saw a sparkling purple leaf falling, and he jumped to his feet and tried to catch it. As before, it simply vanished.

I've seen that before.

Edyn continued onward through the scattered memories within the mist. This time, he ignored their torturous pull, and eventually they began to fade. The ground then turned solid white, and white floating stairs appeared, seemingly weightless, suspended by nothing.

With no other choice, he approached the first stair and took a hesitant step up. More emerged as he climbed, the stairs inclining as they spiraled upward, while a daytime sky took form above.

Edyn climbed until the stairs straightened out and he reached solid ground. Something large loomed on the horizon and he quickened his pace, eager to breach the distance. The closer he came, the more he realized how massive it was.

It appeared to be an ancient city, gleaming entirely in white. Dense flower gardens were scattered high and low on the ancient-looking buildings, some completely covering their bright white surfaces. The mammoth city towered powerfully over Edyn as he neared.

He arrived at its entrance and stopped, looking behind him. Unsurprisingly, nothing was there. Everything had vanished. He faced the mysterious city ahead and knew, at this point, there was no turning back.

12

IRIS OF THE FORGOTTEN

PART I: ETERNITY

Edyn emerged through the grand entrance of the ancient city but stopped himself after just a few short steps, immediately overtaken by the breathtaking setting before him.

The glistening, solid white surfaces of the buildings shone brightly throughout the city's streets. They had carved openings for windows across their various heights, with domed roofs above. Lush green gardens and colorful flowers were scattered everywhere. They filled out portions of the ground level and hung high atop the buildings, some covering entire rooftops and others spilling out of the window openings. Crystal-clear blue skies gleamed overhead, the bright sunlight beaming down and giving everything a natural shimmer. Everything was pristine—even the ground Edyn tread upon.

Amazing.

But for all the majesty of the sprawling city, it gave off a haunting feeling. Something was missing.

Returning his focus, Edyn saw a plaza unfold before him—an open space among the surrounding buildings. An exquisitely crafted fountain stood at its center. Intrigued, he approached the chiseled fountain spewing water high into the air, admiring the radiance of the abandoned city along the way.

It was a fountain from seemingly another time, perfectly matching the rest of the mystical setting. Water spewed from its apex far above and rained down onto a collection of flat asymmetrical surfaces. Edyn reached out to feel the falling ice-cold water.

He saw three paths before him. One street led to the right, bordered with towering buildings. Another led down from the other side of the fountain. On the left were stairs that crept up between rows of buildings adorned with flowers.

As he observed his surroundings, Edyn took notice of several odd things occurring.

Although the city appeared abandoned, he heard the faint echoes of voices and thought he spied figures appearing and disappearing around him. He tried to chase the sounds and images with his ears and eyes, but to no avail.

The sound of children giggling and running up the stairs to his left caught his ear, but he saw nothing. Overtaken by curiosity, he followed the sounds up a winding staircase and ended up in a grassy field filled with fertile gardens. In the middle of the field were two long rows of marbled pillars with a path between them. Each row was connected at the top by hanging vines and vegetation.

He walked between the pillars and onto the path, which appeared to have no end, yet he saw more buildings ahead. Perplexed, he squinted at the illusion and pressed on. The buildings were indeed growing closer, but the path between the columns

12: IRIS OF THE FORGOTTEN

remained unchanged, with no end in sight.

Edyn increased his pace until he was running. The columns zipped past him as he swiftly moved ahead, trying to escape the illusion of an unending path. Eventually, everything abruptly changed.

In an instant, the path underfoot transformed into solid wooden boards, and the columns on either side of him disappeared, replaced by trees of a jungle. A hole formed in the center of the white building ahead, and the wooden path continued into it. Edyn saw more jungle scenery on the other side. He blinked, trying to comprehend what he was looking at.

Determined, he stepped into the circular opening and emerged on the other side. The sounds of unseen wildlife surrounded him.

He was in a dense jungle—the wooden trail winding deeper into it. The temperature was scorching as he progressed through the abundant foliage, walking along the wooden boards that were suspended several feet above the jungle floor.

The path went on for so long that he felt he'd never escape, but that helpless feeling was interrupted by the faint sound of falling water that grew louder and louder. With renewed motivation, he quickened his pace, and before long, reached the source of the sound.

Resting on the edge of a rocky cliff was a shining domed building, a shrine within the dark jungle. A powerful stream flowed just beyond it, ending in a waterfall that crashed over the cliff.

An open doorway in the domed structure invited him to come closer. At the entrance, he pushed aside hanging vines and stepped through into a circular room made of white stone. Torches and strange, ancient-looking symbols, possibly representing letters or words of an unknown language, covered the walls. A larger symbol spanned the entirety of the floor.

AFTERGLOW

When Edyn moved to the center of the room, it began to spin around him, and in the air above, a frightening image of a black, misty entity appeared. Its blurred holographic form took the shape of an indiscernible symbol.

"Who's there?" Edyn said.

I am glad that you have found us
We have been waiting for you

The calm, all-knowing voice echoed throughout the room, engulfing Edyn with its power.

"What? Who are you?"

We are the Forgotten, the Three
We are those who inhabited your world long before your time;
an unfathomable distant past
We were the last of those days
A civilization doomed and, eventually, a race forgotten

"What are you talking about?"

Advancing further than any race before
But our time was running out,
and we had no choice but to find a way to survive
Of course, you would understand
There were only us Three left at that point
And we found a way
To exist in another form
To escape our fate

12: IRIS OF THE FORGOTTEN

Preserving ourselves as data—we transcended
our initial plane of existence

Edyn tried to question the voice but struggled to order his thoughts. Before he could say anything at all, the mysterious entity continued.

Maybe it was a mistake,
but we found a way to continue to exist, forever
Outside of everything else
That is, until He found us

"Who?"

You know Him well
And we are now trapped here in this place, forever
Because He connected to us and then collapsed...
collapsed everything...

This place...
The cloud of memories. The cloud of dream-filled void
After it ended, this is the place where all things now reside
There is no escape
Everything that once was now exists here,
but in the form of scattered memories and dreams
Although, certain things do remain and exist
exactly as they were before
Near where "it" took place

As if knowing what Edyn was thinking, the entity expanded.

AFTERGLOW

Let me be clear: This is not the afterlife. It is very much real
This place is not so different from where you came from
It is, in a way, connected...
But the place you came from, of course, was not actually your home

With those last words spoken, Edyn desperately shouted, "What? You... how do you know?! How do I know you're even real?! If *this* is even real?"

Real? What is real? What is not real?
This place—it is the sum of all thoughts
All things, to be thought of again
Everything that has ever existed was once imagined first
It was once thought of, and so now exists here, only as a memory
And if everything is first imagined, what is real?

"What are you saying?"

*Everything is real. Everything **must** be real*
All thoughts, dreams, memories...
This place—it is all that is left. All that there now can be
If you think of something, then it must exist
It begins to exist somewhere
And that place is here, where the noosphere lingers

Overwhelmed, Edyn's vision blurred, and the entity began to fade from view.
"But you still haven't answered anything! Why am I here?"
Who is thinking of me?

12: IRIS OF THE FORGOTTEN

You won't know me
But there's nothing more we can do
And this might be our only option
We have to try

It'll be like we never knew each other
It wasn't supposed to end like this
What happens next
It doesn't matter
I love you, Edyn

I hope you understood my actions
All we have now is us
And you're all I need, but
I just couldn't go on living like this
It was inevitable
I had to try something
To see if we could have a future

I'm sorry, but
I have to leave you now
It's all my fault, so
Just don't think
There was anything you could have done
This is just how we have to end

We're going to be apart for a long time, but
If you get lost
Come back here

AFTERGLOW

> Just like we promised
> I know you'll be able to find me
>
> Keep me in your memories, Edyn
> This is our goodbye
> But I know I won't lose you forever, because
> You'll still be where you've always been

The hill vanished and, strangely, Edyn was back at the entrance of the ancient city.

How did I end up back here again?

Instinctively, he began walking toward the fountain in the middle of the plaza. Scanning the area, he saw everything was the same as before.

Unsure of what to do, he looked up to the crystal-blue sky in hopes of an answer. His eyes shifted to the right, following the sky against the tops of the tall buildings, until a gap appeared between them. He followed the gap downward until he found himself staring directly at the street that presented itself before him. Resolute, he confirmed his next path of this strange journey.

12: IRIS OF THE FORGOTTEN

PART II: DESTINY

Edyn made his way down the street, creeping between the towering buildings on either side, as he squinted through the rays of a hot sun.

Vacant merchant stands with cloth maroon tops lined the sides of the street, while gusts of wind blew dust and debris through the air and shrouded the view ahead.

He stopped to wipe his eyes and thought he saw apparitions mingling about when he pulled his hands away from his face. He even thought he heard the sounds of a crowd, and children running as they played. But each time he followed the sounds, nothing was there.

Edyn got the feeling he was walking within a once-vibrant place that had long since been abandoned, filled with the memories of the distant past.

He thought about what the entity had told him about this place, and about everything he'd seen here since his arrival through the gates.

"The cloud of memories. The cloud of dream-filled void. The sum of all thoughts."

He moved on, trying to ignore the fleeting sounds and images surrounding him. With each step, the sun sank lower in the sky. Darkness was quickly descending.

He came to the end of the street and saw a circular intersection up ahead. In a grassy field beyond it, a short set of white stone steps led up a small grassy hill. The evening darkness continued its descent as he walked up the steps and underneath a carved stone archway overhead. An eerie feeling came over him as he found himself at the entrance of a cemetery.

He took in the chilling sight of the white stone grave markers and angel statues in view, now with only the final rays of the setting sun reaching them.

Vines and vegetation covered every foot of the cemetery. Angel statues taller than Edyn stared blankly into the distance, their bodies and faces wrapped within the outstretched webs of the green vines, connecting them to one another. Edyn continued his march, moving carefully between them.

He reached the top of the short hill as the black of the evening fully set in. A faint, moonlike glimmer illuminated the cemetery, giving the stones that surrounded him an eerie glow that shone brightly through the darkness.

Ahead, Edyn saw another short set of steps that appeared to lead out of the cemetery, and he walked in their direction.

He took the steps down the hill, exiting the cemetery, and noticed a change in terrain. The ground was sandy here, and he came upon a small wooden boat mere feet from a narrow river. Edyn felt drawn to hop aboard.

The river was calm, barely moving, the moon providing light for the way ahead. Edyn began paddling until he picked up speed and then let the boat glide on its own. He looked to his left and saw the gleaming white city sparkling majestically in the night as he moved slowly past it.

Up ahead was a rounded stone bridge that connected both sides of the river. The bridge inclined and declined steeply for such a short distance, and it gave the appearance of a half oval. The mirror image of the bridge reflected perfectly in the calm water, lit by the moonlight from above.

The reflection of the half oval seemed to extend down below the water's surface, making it look like he was passing through the

12: IRIS OF THE FORGOTTEN

center of a giant eye. He marveled at the sight, and as he floated underneath the bridge, he instinctively crouched as the boat passed through to the other side.

Emerging, he stared in confusion at what lay just ahead. As his boat carried steadily on, it appeared that the river ended abruptly in a plot of grassy land. Edyn coasted the boat up and into the grass until it was firmly planted. Then he gently set the paddle down in the boat and stepped out onto the grass.

He came to a set of stone steps that led down another grassy hill and stopped short, marveling at the sight that lay below. At the bottom of the hill was a small pond with large winding stepping stones leading to a stone building in the middle, as if on an island.

Moonlight shone down on the still water, illuminating the stepping stones. Flowers surrounded the pond, with some of their stray red petals floating atop the water's surface. There was a serenity about it all, and it was unlike anything Edyn had ever seen.

He walked down the short set of steps and approached the pond, listening to the insects chirping in the background. He reached the first circular stepping stone and examined the stone structure ahead. It was a white domed building with green vines hanging down its sides and over an open doorway. Something was glowing in the darkness beyond the entrance.

He stepped onto the first stone. There were ten in all, and they wound back and forth from left to right before reaching the end. When he got there, Edyn stepped through the entrance of the domed structure into a small circular room.

The air was cold, and the room was lit by small torches. Ancient-looking symbols, again appearing to be letters or words of an unknown language, decorated the walls. A larger one covered the entirety of the floor, and Edyn walked onto its center.

Immediately, a cold wind blew, and the room started spinning.

AFTERGLOW

The flames and symbols danced and merged, and Edyn began to feel dizzy. He got the sudden feeling he wasn't alone.

Something above him caught his eye, and as he looked up, he saw a foggy image in the air. It was a black, misty entity like before, appearing to be a hologram, and Edyn could only make out an indiscernible symbol through its blurred form.

A mysterious voice then spoke to him, sounding much like the last.

You have traveled far, child. You must want to know

This time, Edyn stood upright and confidently approached the figure. "What can you tell me about this place?"

This place?
The cloud of memories
The sum of all thoughts
The dream-filled void
All that there was and can be and will be
We are now all but trapped here
Because of Him

"Who? Who are you talking about?"

You should know
The hourglass on its side
He created this
And He connected to us and trapped us here,
like everything else

There was a brief pause before the voice spoke again, as if it

12: IRIS OF THE FORGOTTEN

were dwelling on something.

The threads of fate—we thought we were the ones spinning
But you cannot escape their interwoven design
We, too, learned that

The word "trapped" was still resonating with Edyn. It sent a deep fear coursing through his body. The voice spoke to him as if there was no hope left. "But why? Why can't we do anything about this?"

We are out of time
For there is no more time
There was... an "ending"
Past, present, and future no more
We now exist outside of those laws
In this place, where time itself ceases to exist

Or did we have it wrong all along?
Maybe we viewed its sequence incorrectly
Maybe it was a swaying pendulum
Maybe it was a continuous loop
Maybe it was a spreading mass
Maybe...
But what He did changed it all
Forever

The Omega Point...
A collapsing noosphere...
A spiral collapsing in on itself
This is what happened

AFTERGLOW

This is why we are all here together
Why we <u>can</u> all be here together

Edyn struggled to process what was being said. Before he could gather his thoughts, the voice continued.

But you should not be concerned as much with what this place is,
but rather, who you are
A wanderer
A lingering dream
One of the Last
A similar race, and fate, as our own
From a time that was not to be

At those words, Edyn dropped to the floor, overcome with powerful emotions. Pain shot through his body, straight to his core, and the room spun around him. The voice closed with one final statement that reverberated deep within Edyn's fragile mind.

The fleeting dust of crumbling ruins, you are...

Chills coursed through Edyn as he writhed in anguish, suffering through stray fragments of distant memories. He drifted away, lost within his mind, and returned to a familiar scene.

12: IRIS OF THE FORGOTTEN

I know what you're thinking
This won't be the end
You won't know me
But there's nothing more we can do
And this might be our only option
We have to try

It'll be like we never knew each other
It wasn't supposed to end like this
What happens next
It doesn't matter
I love you, Edyn

I hope you understood my actions
All we have now is us
And you're all I need, but
I just couldn't go on living like this
It was inevitable
I had to try something
To see if we could have a future

I'm sorry, but
I have to leave you now
It's all my fault, so
Just don't think
There was anything you could have done
This is just how we have to end

We're going to be apart for a long time, but
If you get lost

AFTERGLOW

>Come back here
>Just like we promised
>I know you'll be able to find me
>
>Keep me in your memories, Edyn
>This is our goodbye
>But I know I won't lose you forever, because
>You'll still be where you've always been

The memory vanished and Edyn came to his senses. Heavy rain fell all around him as light and images took form. He stood in shock as he scanned the area. For the third time, he was back at the entrance of the ancient city. All was the same as before except for the storm that raged and replaced the crystal-blue skies with dark and ominous clouds.

He took a few wet and heavy steps into the plaza, the familiar fountain now overflowing, and hopelessly looked up to the sky above. With nowhere to escape to, it appeared Edyn's journey through this mysterious place was not yet finished.

12: IRIS OF THE FORGOTTEN

PART III: REALITY

Rain washed down over Edyn's face. After a few moments of respite, he opened his eyes. The gray and dreary weather cast an eerie look over the ancient buildings, diminishing the radiance they had once shown. From this plaza, there was only one route he hadn't taken, and that was the street that led down past the other side of the fountain.

Edyn made a wide half-circle around the fountain as it violently overflowed from the heavy rain and approached the street directly ahead. For the third time now, Edyn chose his path, and with so many questions running through his mind, hoped this one would lead him to answers.

He splashed down the wet street, white, garden-filled buildings on either side of him—the lush greenery bringing a sense of life to the gray and otherwise gloomy atmosphere. Eventually, the road wound into another circular plaza bordered with small buildings, with a road on the opposite end of the plaza continuing onward.

Edyn examined the structures as the rain began to fall harder. Before long, he noticed something odd happening, and he wondered whether his eyes were playing tricks on him. The structures were changing—deteriorating right before his eyes.

Bright flashes of lightning swept through the area while loud cracks of thunder boomed, and with each, the buildings became increasingly more run-down. A deafening thunderclap struck, followed by a blinding lightning flash, and Edyn shielded his eyes.

Once he felt safe to uncover them, he stood in shock at the sight ahead. All the buildings were now in a completely ruined state—some crumbled, some on their sides, others with sections missing. The previously lush vegetation was now lying in a state of decay.

The storm continued to rage and intensify in strength. Edyn grew frightened. With the destruction all around him and the road ahead blocked with debris, there seemed to be nowhere to escape.

He darted through the plaza, avoiding the fallen debris and trying to find entry for shelter in any of the buildings.

Just as a feeling of hopelessness descended, a large, partially deteriorated building caught his eye. Although the doorway on the ground level was blocked, there were railed steps leading up to the second floor, which had an open archway. The thunder and rain intensified as Edyn rushed forward, grabbed onto the railing, and sped up the steps and under cover.

He found himself within the second-floor hallway of an open, square-shaped room. From here he could view down into the rest of it, protected by a still-standing railing. Much of the room was in shambles, and was entirely bare. To his left were stone steps leading down to the first floor, but there was a large section missing in the middle. Only the top and bottom steps remained.

Looking farther down the hall, he saw a doorway that led to another room. Edyn decided to give it a look. Being careful with his steps on the unstable floor, he ventured down the long hallway as the sound of rainfall increased.

The closer he came to the doorway, the louder the rain became, as if the door led directly outside. He stepped through the door into a large open room and got an explanation. Most of the roof was missing, allowing the rain to waterfall in.

Edyn walked up to a railing and looked down to the first-story floor and saw a large, circular pool of water coming up from underground. There didn't appear to be any direct way down, as much of the second floor was destroyed, but there was a part of

12: IRIS OF THE FORGOTTEN

the railing missing nearby, and he walked over to it, transfixed by an inviting glow in the pool below.

Watching his step, he crouched down at the section of the railing that was missing and looked below. Large pieces of the deteriorated building were stacked just beneath his feet, and Edyn used them to climb down.

Standing in the area exposed by the missing roof, he approached the overflowing pool and examined it. Where at first it had appeared shallow, now he could see it led much deeper, as if it were an underwater tunnel. A glowing light came from deep within.

With all fear lost and nowhere else to go, Edyn held his breath, dropped into the water, and began swimming downward.

He swam into the underground tunnel, led by the glowing light in view directly ahead. He saw the end of the tunnel in the near distance and increased his pace. The tunnel opened up into a larger pool of water. Its surface was illuminated brightly overhead.

Swimming up toward the light, Edyn broke the water's surface and took a deep, gasping inhale as he pulled back his hair. The edge of the pool he was treading in ran into a dirt ground surface just ahead, and he swam toward it.

He pulled himself up and out of the frigid water and wiped the water away from his eyes. The sounds of wildlife rang loudly around him as he examined his surroundings. He appeared to be outdoors within a dense, green forest, but there was a ceiling in view high above with bright streaks of light shining down from it. Edyn wondered how he could have ended up in such a different-looking place so quickly.

Towering above him were tall, white, vine-covered statues tangled within the trees and vegetation. Edyn felt intimidated as he walked past the mammoth, humanlike statues that stood so high their feet were taller than him.

Looking up, he grew perplexed when he saw what was causing the bright streaks of light that were shining down from above. The "ceiling" high above looked to be made of dirt, and it was riddled with cracks. Bright sunlight shone through the cracks, casting beams of light against and past the heads of the statues. It gave Edyn the feeling that he was within underground ruins just below the Earth's surface.

He traversed the forest, brushing vines and vegetation away from his face as the sounds of wildlife grew louder. A white, domed temple covered in green vines appeared in an opening just ahead. The light from above shone down brightly on it, as if it were being presented.

An open doorway invited Edyn closer, and the glow of the building grew as he neared. When he reached the threshold, he walked between the low-hanging vines in the doorway and stepped inside.

Again, Edyn found himself within a mysterious white room with unknown, ancient-looking symbols scattered on the walls and a large one spanning the entirety of the floor. The room was well lit, with sunlight shining through the many windows spanning high across the tops of the walls.

Edyn approached the center of the room, but after only a few steps, he stopped short. The room was quickly growing brighter, the light entering the windows rapidly intensifying.

The light increased so much that soon Edyn was blind to anything but the white light. He grew dizzy and his eyes strained as he tried to squint through it. He felt a twinge of fear, the same as if he were standing in complete darkness.

That fear only grew when he got the distinct feeling he wasn't alone.

12: IRIS OF THE FORGOTTEN

Moments later, the misty, holographic figure of an indiscernible black symbol made its way through the light. The entity, with its calm and all-knowing voice, spoke.

Time
Here, it stands still
But it is time
The time for you to know

Edyn listened in silence, intrigued and hopeful about what he might learn.

You are here for the same reasons as us
You tried to escape, but He found you too, and He brought you here
We are all trapped, together
The never-ending spiral of memories...
It is because of Him—the hourglass on its side
He became all but a god
And He created His own Heaven
But, of course, you would know all of that

Something about the description of whoever this entity was talking about made Edyn think and feel that he did, in fact, know all of that, and he got lost within his mind.

"*The hourglass on its side...*"

A sharp pain shot through Edyn's head, accompanied by piercing electrical sounds and flashes of distant memories.

Terrified and in agony, he fell to his knees.

AFTERGLOW

You don't remember Him?
You will meet Him soon enough

"Who—" Edyn tried, but he was unable to speak.

But of course you can't remember
You have "traveled" in ways no other has
A fragile mind...
Your subconscious has all but deteriorated
Your memories, shattered and scrambled
Poor child
Do not fear
It would be impossible for it to be otherwise

A chill of fear coursed through Edyn. Deep inside, something was telling him there was truth to the words being spoken to him.

You are a lost memory
One from a place that was not to be
And ended up in a place you shouldn't have been
A memory who was lost within a memory
While being lost within your own memories
And now, have come to exist here
The place where all memories reside

Edyn recalled something Raine had said to him.
"*At what point in time does a memory exist? Where do memories reside?*"

12: IRIS OF THE FORGOTTEN

One of the Last...
A race with similar ambitions as our own
From a world long since perished
It is futile to deny it
This is your reality

"That cannot be!"

Edyn writhed on the ground as his vision blurred and fragments of fleeting images flashed through his mind: a dying, desolate area with pillars of blue light beaming up to the sky; strange machinery within a dark building; and an ominous chamber with an intense blue light emanating from within.

Now go
Through where the remains of time rests
And the places beyond
Much still exists just as it were in those places
Near where "it" occurred
Find Him
Confront your existence

Edyn drifted away deeper within his mind as the words of the entity faded and were soon replaced by the haunting words of a crying woman.

It's possible we can be together again

I know what you're thinking
This won't be the end
You won't know me

AFTERGLOW

But there's nothing more we can do
And this might be our only option
We have to try

It'll be like we never knew each other
It wasn't supposed to end like this
What happens next
It doesn't matter
I love you, Edyn

I hope you understood my actions
All we have now is us
And you're all I need, but
I just couldn't go on living like this
It was inevitable
I had to try something
To see if we could have a future

I'm sorry, but
I have to leave you now
It's all my fault, so
Just don't think
There was anything you could have done
This is just how we have to end

We're going to be apart for a long time, but
If you get lost
Come back here
Just like we promised
I know you'll be able to find me

12: IRIS OF THE FORGOTTEN

> Keep me in your memories, Edyn
> This is our goodbye
> But I know I won't lose you forever, because
> You'll still be where you've always been

The memory faded and clear vision returned to Edyn, the ancient city now far behind him. It was night, and he was out in the open. The wind howled and fog twisted about the cold darkness, concealing what lay ahead. Unwavering, he pressed on.

A fierce gust of wind sent a cloud of dust flying through the air and into Edyn's eyes. He shielded them momentarily, but once uncovered, saw a colossal structure taking form high above.

Just ahead, through the curling fog, a dark tower loomed.

13

TIME'S FORTRESS

Edyn approached the tower, its form tangled within the webs of fog and darkness. Glimmers of light were suspended in the air near it, glowing brightly through the black.

He increased his pace through the barren, open plain, as he shielded his eyes from the blowing sand.

He arrived at the base of the tower and viewed a set of wide stone steps that led upward. Walking up the massive stone steps, he was able to discern the source of the glimmers of light.

Both sides of the steps were lined with hourglasses on their sides, suspended in the air at eye level. Edyn saw bright light emitting from the golden sand within—an even amount on both sides—with a connecting strain hovering in the center. He continued up the steps, the light from the hourglasses guiding the way.

As he neared the top, he began to feel the weight of the tower within him. It felt as if there were an invisible force swaying back and forth, engulfing everything in its path.

There was a consistency to its pattern and a deep ringing accompanying each sway, not audible to the ears but felt deep inside. He braced through this phenomenon as it steadily intensified in power, and reached the top step.

Now at the foot of what towered over him, daylight cracked through the darkness, revealing the timeworn structure looming above. There were a mass of towers, pathways, stairs, and ramparts as far as his eye could see. It was masterfully crafted but lacked symmetry, and it branched out in all directions.

Its form was comprised of a dark-gray stone and had windowlike openings scattered throughout. Dark steel bars crossed their apertures.

Edyn began to see this place for what it really was—a fortress. A protector of what lay beyond.

Before him, a tall, enclosed hallway presented itself, leading inside. He advanced toward the hall, but before entering he saw a small pool of dark water surrounded by a barrier of chiseled gray stone. He went to it and peered down.

The water, so dark it almost looked black, was still. In the dim glow of the sky above, Edyn's face reflected back.

Just then, the figure of a woman came into view beside his reflection, hovering just over his shoulder. He saw her face vividly as she stared longingly at him.

Serah?

He spun around, but she wasn't there.

He quickly turned back to the water below. Strangely, it rippled on its own, blurring the mirage of her face. Once still again, only Edyn's lone reflection stared back.

Edyn felt deflated, struggling to piece together his thoughts. What was real, and what wasn't? Where was he? Seeing Serah's reflection only deepened his confusion.

Was she even real?

He picked himself up and set his sights on the colossal structure before him. With renewed determination, he marched into the

13: TIME'S FORTRESS

vast, windowless hallway that led inside, the glow of light disappearing with each step.

Although the hall appeared to lead nowhere, he pressed on through the increasing darkness. Finally, he saw a faint light coming from just ahead. It was coming from the cracks of a door.

The door was made of stone and was without a handle. Feeling around, his hand fell upon a cut-in piece he could latch onto. Using all his strength, he slid it open. Dust and stone pieces fell from above, as if the door hadn't been opened in ages. Light poured through as it opened.

He arrived within a large open room that left him in a state of shock. Scattered fragments of mirrors—in all shapes and sizes—covered the entire back wall. It appeared as if it had once been a giant mirror that had shattered into hundreds of broken pieces. Edyn approached slowly, the mirrors projecting numerous reflections from different angles.

What followed next roused feelings of pain within him. Dozens of distant memories from Edyn's past played out in the mirrors, each lasting only a mere fraction of a second before being replaced by the next. They all appeared as one grand image, broken up by the many scattered pieces. Voices and sounds echoed through the room, only to be swiftly replaced by the next memory before Edyn could process them. The memories stirred intense emotions he hadn't experienced since long ago. Overwhelmed, he sank to his knees. He pressed his palms on the floor, tilted his head downward, and closed his eyes so he wouldn't have to bear through the memories any longer.

When he cracked open his eyes, he figured the memories cycling through the mirrors must have stopped because he was no longer perceiving movement from one image to the next. Slowly, he turned his head up to look and confirmed his suspicion. The flashing images had ceased, leaving only one.

I know this place.

He saw the image of a dying, desolate place. Orange dirt covered the barren land, and clouds of orange dust flew through the air. Small, crumbled buildings filled the area, worn down and in ruins, yet with beams of bright-blue light emitting from them—pillars of light reaching high into the sky above.

Pulling himself up to his feet, he approached the wall of mirrors. Orange dust was coming from the place imprisoned within them, and it circulated throughout the room. He could even feel the scorching heat of the sun radiating at the top of the image. He felt a glimmer of hope as he drew closer to this haunting, familiar place.

He was almost close enough to touch it when the wall of mirrors suddenly shattered. He jumped back as the mirrors disintegrated into a million tiny pieces, crashing loudly to the floor, the place that was before him now unreachable.

Why...

In place of the mirrors stood an open doorway. It emitted a bright, inviting glow. Casting his feelings aside, he passed through it into a bright and mostly empty room. Everything in it—the walls, ceiling, floor, and a lone desk—were white, devoid of color.

Edyn moved to the white desk that sat in the middle of the room as a loud gonging sound rang somewhere in the distance. There was a blank canvas on the desk encased in a white picture frame, and a paintbrush lying to the side. On the other side of the canvas, a pendulum swayed slowly, clicking with each motion. He saw that it coincided with the powerful force he'd felt swaying back and forth throughout this place and within him since arriving.

He looked past the desk to an open balcony with black steel railings on the far side of the room. A cold chill hit him as he approached it. He looked out, now much higher in the tower. A

13: TIME'S FORTRESS

loud, repetitive sound pulsed all around. The sky above was gray and cloudy, with light cracking through in spots, and a cold wind blew. There were paths and stairways scattered everywhere in all directions, with sections of the structure connected by them. Down below was a courtyard that looked to be the center of the entire fortress.

Directly ahead stood a colossal building with an enormous clock tower stretching high in the sky, watching over and acting as the centerpiece to all. The face of the clock had a faint yellow glow. Its hands were missing, and it was marked with unknown symbols in place of numbers. Edyn finally identified the source of the repetitive force felt throughout this entire place—the clock was gonging endlessly, its sound filling the whole of the fortress.

The balcony where he stood continued to the right and all the way around to the other side, connecting to the body of the clock tower, and Edyn felt drawn to it.

He traveled toward the clock tower under outstretched sections of the fortress, their chiseled stone surfaces catching the light from above and casting shadows below, as the gonging intensified. When he reached the foot of the tower, he walked up a short set of steps to a stone door.

Instead of a doorknob or handle to slide it open, the door had a weathered, timeworn stone wheel. Edyn grabbed onto the dusty handles of the spokes and tried to turn it clockwise. It wouldn't budge. He tried the other direction, and with some effort, it began to move. Edyn thrust down forcibly. He jumped backward when the wheel spun freely on its own and the door slowly opened.

He stepped into a dark room and heard a loud crash as the door slammed shut behind him. A staircase was all that filled the room's dark-gray walls, its silver steps suspended in the air and leading directly up to an open doorway above.

With no other option, he walked up the floating steps. An uneasy feeling of weightlessness came over him as he progressed, feeling smaller and more vulnerable the higher he climbed.

At the top step, he reached a larger platform with the open doorway. He stepped through and found himself within a white, narrow corridor. The floor, ceiling, and back wall of the passage were bright white, and there were floor-to-ceiling glass windows spanning both of its sides. But most captivating was what was protruding from the back wall: a spiral of varying fluorescent colors reaching out toward him.

Have I seen this before?

Edyn drew closer and noticed the spiral was comprised of shiny, colorful orbs connected to dark steel arms that extended out from the back wall, and as he neared, saw that it was spinning ever so slightly. It seemed to be the gears of the clock tower—and possibly the core of the entire fortress.

The colors churned, giving the illusion of an advancing spiral. Intrigued, he reached for the closest colorful orb as it slowly spun, feeling its energy. With a slight downward thrust of his hand, he sent it spinning faster.

The spiral picked up speed and Edyn heard clicking sounds, as if something had been activated. It accelerated so much that the spiral's spectrum of colors could no longer be distinguished, forming a blurry mass engulfing the passage like blotches of paint spreading on a canvas.

The intensity of the spinning and spreading colors overtook Edyn's eyes and he shielded them. The corridor felt like it was changing and expanding.

Finally, moments later, it abruptly ceased, and the merged colors took on a new, grand form. With his mouth gaping open and deep feelings intensifying within him, Edyn opened his eyes to

13: TIME'S FORTRESS

the finished product that presented itself.

Spanning before him was the dying, desolate place that lay in ruins. Worn-down structures and barren land within the orange dirt of a decaying environment surrounded him. Beams of bright-blue light shot up high into the sky above.

This place…

I…

Edyn stumbled backward in fear as feelings of recognition began to surface.

Am I…?

Familiar voices rang in his head:

"One of the Last."
"You are a lost memory."
"One from a place that was not to be."
"The fleeting dust of crumbling ruins, you are…"

He covered his ears, desperately trying to shake off the voices and the realization that was stirring within him.

No.

That can't be possible.

His vision blurred, and he faded away into a memory.

I'm not sure where you and I will end up
But I know, from everything we've learned,
It's possible we can be together again

I know what you're thinking
This won't be the end
You won't know me

AFTERGLOW

But there's nothing more we can do
And this might be our only option
We have to try

It'll be like we never knew each other
It wasn't supposed to end like this
What happens next
It doesn't matter
I love you, Edyn

I hope you understood my actions
All we have now is us
And you're all I need, but
I just couldn't go on living like this
It was inevitable
I had to try something
To see if we could have a future

I'm sorry, but
I have to leave you now
It's all my fault, so
Just don't think
There was anything you could have done
This is just how we have to end

We're going to be apart for a long time, but
If you get lost
Come back here
Just like we promised
I know you'll be able to find me

13: TIME'S FORTRESS

> Keep me in your memories, Edyn
> This is our goodbye
> But I know I won't lose you forever, because
> You'll still be where you've always been

The memory vanished and Edyn found himself outside, the rear of the fortress now behind him as if he had passed through it. This confused him, but not as much as what he'd just witnessed.

Who am I?

He was in a barren, hazy space. Fierce winds whipped up clouds of orange dust. The sun blazed overhead, casting the landscape in harsh light. He could see nothing beyond the immediate area where he stood, as if it were separated from the expanse beyond, which was blurred in an eerie, distorted state.

He pressed on, and when the flying dust died down, faintly made out a building that lay just ahead. He approached the building, still intact but in a decaying state, with only its entrance area in focus.

Something about this place felt different from all the other places he'd journeyed through. It felt more real. A chilling feeling descended upon him as he recalled what the last entity had told him.

"Now go, through where the remains of time rests, and the places beyond. Much still exists just as it were in those places, near where 'it' occurred."

He dwelled on those words as he examined the face of the building, smooth and white with blue accents. Despite the state it was in, the design had a modern appearance.

AFTERGLOW

A broken sign hung diagonally above the entranceway. Some of the first letters were missing, but squinting through the cloudy haze, Edyn was able to make out the rest:

Research Center

14
CHRYSALIS RESEARCH CENTER

The doors of the entrance mysteriously creaked open on their own. They seemed to react to Edyn's very presence. Guided by curiosity, he stepped through.

The interior was sleek and modern, with white, gleaming floors and walls, accented by faint blue and green lighting. Windows lined the walls and stretched across the ceiling, flooding the space with natural light. Edyn was overwhelmed at the sight before him. He felt a strong sense of familiarity here.

He was in a lobby filled with modern-looking chairs and benches. Ahead of him was a large front desk with a short wall behind it.

On either side of the desk, wide sets of steps led upward to a higher level within the open lobby area. There were monitors scattered on the surrounding walls—some broken, others displaying brightly lit but illegible symbols.

Above the desk, large, illuminated letters spelled out the name of the hall, with a smaller quote displayed beneath it:

AFTERGLOW

Chrysalis Research Center
May its ethereal existence be unending and never fleeting, this Flower of Life

    Hovering above the name, the symbol of the research center appeared as a colorful hologram projected in midair. It consisted of thirteen circles—six outer and seven inner—connected by radiant lines, each glowing with a spectrum of shifting lights.

Metatron's Cube.

But why is it here?

    Edyn advanced through the lobby and saw faint sparkling objects suspended in the air at eye level—orbs of golden energy about the size of his fist. He reached out to touch one but before he could, it reacted, momentarily glowing brighter as if activated, then expanding in size.

    A large projection with glowing lines of text appeared before him—their words revealing a mysterious conversation.

How long have we been working in here?
It feels like an eternity, and I'm drained.
I know there isn't much left out there,
but I feel like... I don't know...

                                          I know what you mean.
           Like we should be spending our remaining time differently.

Right.
I know we have to keep going, but these are our lives too.
And it's just... the way things are looking...
I'm not sure if any of it is going to work anyways, you know?
I just feel like...

14: CHRYSALIS RESEARCH CENTER

> I know. I've had the same thoughts lately too.
> I'd rather be somewhere else.
> Not stuck here in Chrysalis.

Exactly.

> Wait! Why are you...?
> He can see these, can't He?

Of course He can. He sees everything.
Sorry, I'll end it.
I just think we should leave as many of these as possible at this point.
You never know.

○─────────────────────────────

The projection ended and immediately contracted back to its original form. Edyn stepped away, confused.

What was that?

There were many more glowing orbs scattered throughout the grand hall, casting a shimmering golden sparkle, and he was eager to continue. As he moved toward the desk, another orb drifted closer to him and expanded.

○─────────────────────────────

The electrical nature of the brain,
and the electrical signals passed across itself via its synapses—
it's all not so different from computing.

And our thoughts, our memories, our consciousness...
It's becoming clear that we're connected in these ways.
It's all starting to tie together.

But how can we use this for the projects?

I'll need to run the latest data through Adriel.
If there's something in there that we can use,
He'll know.

⊙────────────────────────────

Now, even closer to the desk, Edyn activated another.

⊙────────────────────────────

I know I shouldn't be taking a break,
but I just need to clear my head.
I still can't figure it out.
Time—its sequence…
I'm so close. But I'm at a wall.
I know we still have a good group researching
within the other departments,
but I just wish there was more I could do with this.

It's funny, actually. The time we think we still have.
You never know when that might change.
If nothing else, I at least know that.

⊙────────────────────────────

What are they talking about?
It was evident that these were records left by the people who once worked here, and Edyn was eager to learn more.

He arrived at the front desk. Monitors sat atop it and were attached to the wall behind it. All displayed varying jumbled data and indiscernible symbols.

14: CHRYSALIS RESEARCH CENTER

Above, the name of the research center and the projection of Metatron's Cube shone brightly.

Edyn chose the stairway on the right of the desk. Flashing blue lights lined the stair railing, and a sparkling golden light floated in the air nearby.

It's crazy to think that the decline began centuries ago.
Where did we go wrong?
If only we had paid more attention at first,
maybe it could have been prevented.
And now, somehow, we're all that's left.
Everyone that still *is* is here.
There is no more.
I still can't fathom it.

And how did *we* get so lucky?
Life still remains in this area.
What made this place, and us, so special?

Unless there *are* others left, somewhere out there.
There has been speculation about that.
But with our planet's condition, there would be no way to know.
But it doesn't matter anymore.
It is useless to wonder.
We must figure this out.
And we have to hurry.

If he truly was the last one—
we're running out of time.

AFTERGLOW

The log closed and Edyn reached the top of the stairs, now a floor up, but still within the open lobby area. More glowing orbs floated at the top of the climb.

Do you think I'll be able to see them again if any of this works?

I'm not sure.
I don't think any of us know the answer to that.

I've just been thinking lately...
The connection.
Our thoughts.
It's almost like an invisible atmosphere.
At least, that's what it appears like in the
initial images we've been able to create.
So maybe...

Yeah,
Adriel has been mentioning something along those lines too.
And He's been obsessing over one specific aspect of it:
A spiral.
He's talking about it for other things too.
Everything spiraling.

Well, there does appear to be that type of flow in regard to time,
especially when we speed up the imagery and projections of the Waves.
They've actually tested out some of our findings downstairs,
and even they are seeing similar results.
But what's weird is, from what they've seen,
the flow seems to slow down the further out they project it.

14: CHRYSALIS RESEARCH CENTER

                                                           That's strange.

Yeah, it is. I…

                                                           No, I mean,
it's strange that Adriel didn't mention anything about that to me.
I figure, if they are seeing those results,
then He obviously already has, too.

Really? He didn't? That's odd.
But let's get back in there and run more tests to be sure.
You know, everything with this is so delicate.
We have to be careful.

                                                                   Right…

What's the matter?

                                          It's just… I can't shake this feeling.
Why wouldn't He mention that?
And it's not just that.
There's been other things with Him lately, too.
I just get the feeling…

Don't talk like that.
I trust Him.

                                                       I do too. It's just…
I'm starting to wonder.

Edyn stared down a sleek gray hallway with bright overhead

lights, doors lining either side, and a large glass double door at the end. As he approached the first door on his right, it slid open automatically. Inside was a small dark room with a desk covered by research prints and electrical equipment. A lone bright light near the desk drew him in.

All our research, and any of the possibilities—
all of it still depends on Adriel.
It is meaningless without Him.
Only He can take things where we need them to go.

After my people recovered and consolidated all of the knowledge and technology that survived the calamities,
they created Him—the pinnacle of artificial intelligence.
A self-governing and self-regulating energy—
the technological core of this entire research center—
that could help advance and accelerate our efforts.

But it's clear—He is far more than that now.
And we are almost solely relying on Him at this point.
If we *can* use the Cube, and if there *is* a way to ascend,
or even if we are relegated to using the Fail-Safe—
He would be the one to figure it out.

It has been truly remarkable to witness His progress since His creation.
His ability to self-develop over time—
yes, with us guiding and pushing Him—
has yielded results far beyond what we could have hoped for.
It is now quite evident, at this rate, that His intelligence
will far surpass anything we could have ever dreamt possible.

14: CHRYSALIS RESEARCH CENTER

But with this, of course, there will be risks.
He is all but a truly living being now.
And the level He will inevitably reach—
it's not only beyond our comprehension,
it's also well beyond our control.
I know we don't have the time or resources
to be able to focus on any of that.
We don't have much of a choice at this point anyways.
But one must wonder about the possibilities.

Adriel—I think I know him.

Edyn left the room and entered the next one farther down the hallway. Covering the desks and scattered on the walls were sketches of different variations of Metatron's Cube.

Immersed by the symbols surrounding him, Edyn moved toward the back of the room, where something was emitting a bright light. A small structure stood at the rear, and a colorful projection of the Cube hovered above it.

It was a hologram projection just like the one in the lobby, and its dimensions could be viewed in full as it rotated slowly, as if on an axis. The interconnected circles and streaking lines created magnificent shapes and angles, making it appear as if it were an optical illusion.

Moving close, something caught his attention from the corner of his eye.

We've come so far, and have learned so much.
We've deciphered so many of its secrets.
The most sacred of all the ancient geometry.

AFTERGLOW

Could it really take us to that place?
Could we complete and actually *initiate* the Transcendence?

We may be close, and yet, it seems like it may be futile.
The chances of it working are slim.
I feel the alternative will inevitably be our most likely outcome.

The so-called "Fail-Safe."
The memory generation.
It is now becoming much closer to an actual possibility.
Adriel is attaining an energy efficiency
far greater than we ever thought possible.
And it just might be enough
to provide the computational efficacy to power it.
But should we rejoice in this?
If we do end up activating it,
it would mean that the other projects had failed,
and we had but no other choice.
And yes, it would be something. Something spectacular.
But it would be nothing more than an illusion.

Regardless of the outcome, I believe we must hurry.
Our remaining resources here are dwindling,
and the wasteland that awaits us all is fast approaching.

The log closed and Edyn dwelled on everything he had discovered upon entering this place. It resonated with him in ways he couldn't quite understand, stirring troubling thoughts and feelings.

Out of nowhere, a strong sense of fear overcame him, as if a horrifying realization was coming to light. He staggered backward

14: CHRYSALIS RESEARCH CENTER

toward the door and stumbled out of the room. Struggling to balance, he braced himself against the wall of the corridor as he made his way down it, and returned to a place deep within his fragile mind.

We didn't think everything through
And we have only ourselves to blame
How did I not see this coming?

I'm not sure where you and I will end up
But I know, from everything we've learned,
It's possible we can be together again

I know what you're thinking
This won't be the end
You won't know me
But there's nothing more we can do
And this might be our only option
We have to try

It'll be like we never knew each other
It wasn't supposed to end like this
What happens next
It doesn't matter
I love you, Edyn

I hope you understood my actions
All we have now is us
And you're all I need, but
I just couldn't go on living like this

AFTERGLOW

It was inevitable
I had to try something
To see if we could have a future

I'm sorry, but
I have to leave you now
It's all my fault, so
Just don't think
There was anything you could have done
This is just how we have to end

We're going to be apart for a long time, but
If you get lost
Come back here
Just like we promised
I know you'll be able to find me

Keep me in your memories, Edyn
This is our goodbye
But I know I won't lose you forever, because
You'll still be where you've always been

Edyn was fixated on the frosted glass double doors before him, with slim corridors branching to the left and to the right, seeming to circle the room the doors led to.

There was something frighteningly familiar about the doors, and he felt as if something inside was trying to warn him as he peered up to a steel-engraved sign above:

Replication Monitoring

14: CHRYSALIS RESEARCH CENTER

Ignoring his hesitancy and fear, Edyn reached out and pushed the doors open. The moment he stepped through, he was overwhelmed by powerful emotions coursing through him—a mix of pain and sadness—as scattered thoughts and distant memories tried to make their way through.

Why am I feeling like this?

Edyn did his best to push aside the growing despair and scanned the chilling room. It was a highly advanced place with many desks scattered throughout, monitors and data storage devices filling them. It had the same sleek design as the rest of Chrysalis with hints of green and blue accents and was illuminated by overhead lights.

But what was most striking was what lay at the center of it all: a separate square-shaped room with glass walls bordering its entire perimeter, offering a view inside from all sides.

Edyn studied the room, sealed off and enclosed in glass, and picked up on something. The desks, machines, and monitors all appeared to be individual stations, and all of them were facing this mysterious room in the middle.

There was a steel doorway on the side of the glass wall facing him. It was shut and locked with a strong steel latch, with multiple electronic devices appearing to provide additional security and locking access. It was clear that whatever was contained within this room was not only being observed, but possibly *protected*.

Edyn moved in for a closer look. There wasn't much contained within the glass-encased room, and it gave the appearance of having been abandoned long ago. All that remained was a bare bed with strange machinery above it hanging from the ceiling, and a few monitoring devices nearby.

He continued to the next side of the sealed room and came to a large observation desk that appeared as if it were the main one of this entire place, residing only a few feet away from the glass. A monitor hovered just above the desk's surface, and Edyn made his way over to it, viewing it from the station's point of view.

Standing at the desk, he reached out for the floating device. It activated.

The screen illuminated, its contents appearing to be interactive. Glowing boxes with bright-orange borders filled the screen. They looked like selectable buttons, but most were errored out, overlayed with indecipherable symbols, their borders jagged and inconsistent.

Edyn scrolled down with his fingers until he came across one that could be selected, and touched it. He heard a faint beeping while the orange outline of the glowing box flickered, indicating it had been activated, before expanding to fill the entire screen. Unlike the text logs he had encountered thus far, a video recording began to play, and the sound of a young woman's voice was heard.

———————— ▲ ▼ ⁄ ⁞ ————————

Look at her. How innocent.
She has no idea just how important she is.
It isn't fair to her to bear such a burden.
But there she is, oblivious to it all.

———————— ▲ ▼ ⁄ ⁞ ————————

Edyn stood in shock. The video showed the very observation room before him, but from some time in the distant past. There was a small bed filled with a child's bedding and enclosed by a protective barrier. Machinery hung from the ceiling as it did now, and similar monitoring devices stood nearby. But what shocked Edyn most was what was being shown a few feet away from the bed, on the floor.

14: CHRYSALIS RESEARCH CENTER

Facing away from the camera, a toddler sat and played contentedly with her toys.

––––––––––––––––––– ▲▼ʏ≡ –––––––––––––––––––

I will fully dedicate myself to her, this sweet child,
for as many years as I have left.
Not just to examine and study, but to teach.
We have to teach her everything—all our knowledge.
We don't have much time—
to do it this way.
To keep the real world.

––––––––––––––––––– ▲▼ʏ≡ –––––––––––––––––––

The video ended and immediately collapsed back to the main screen. An unsettling feeling crept within Edyn.

Something didn't feel right.

No...

He scrolled down the screen, eager to discover more. He found another colored box and jabbed the air with his finger to trigger it.

Another video began to play. It was of the same observation room, but this time the girl in the recording was older, about five years old, with short black hair. She was sitting at the edge of her bed with her head facing the floor. The voice of the young woman spoke again.

––––––––––––––––––– ▲▼ʏ≡ –––––––––––––––––––

"What am I?"
She asked me that today after one of our tests,
and she's just been sitting there like that for hours ever since.
I was so shocked. I didn't know what to say.
I guess we haven't really prepared for something like that just yet.
How could a child so young even think to ask such a question?

AFTERGLOW

And it wasn't just that. It was the *way* she asked.
She seemed sad about it.
And she seems sad now, like she's missing something.
Lately, she's been displaying feelings and emotions just like *us*.

There used to be a debate about whether that would be the case,
and truthfully, myself included,
most thought she might be more of an empty vessel.
But it's become clear that isn't the case.
I now think it's possible she may be exactly like us on the inside.
When she grabbed my hand today during that test,
and the way she looked at me,
I could just feel it.

―――――――――― ⋏ ▽ ⅄ ⋮ ――――――――――

The video ended and again reverted back to the main screen. Edyn's feelings were intensifying. Something within felt as if it were ready to burst.

That can't... Could she...?

He saw another selectable box just below the last. His hand trembled as he reached out to touch it. It felt as if some truth was about to come to light.

The video began to play, this time displaying a dim version of the observation room lit only by a faint glowing light. The child lay on her back, asleep in bed. Edyn pulled closer to the screen, eager to get a better look at the child's face. And just as the woman began to speak, Edyn became overwhelmed with emotion. The child's face looked familiar.

―――――――――― ⋏ ▽ ⅄ ⋮ ――――――――――

I've been feeling a bit down today, so apologies for sounding cynical.
It's just... we've put so much into this. We had to.

14: CHRYSALIS RESEARCH CENTER

After we lost our ability to reproduce,
synthetically created humans were our only option to try to survive.
Creations that would then be, to the best of our abilities,
genetically engineered to perfection.

But it has been, by all accounts, a monumental failure.
The negligent success rate, the resources exhausted,
and the time we've wasted.
Maybe we should have spent our energy and effort elsewhere.
And now…
Now our time is quickly evaporating.

But there she lies, ever so peacefully.
To this very day, the only one who ever survived. A miracle.
How did this one make it?
And why can't we get it to work again?

At least we have her. Our only hope.
If this world does survive after all,
as long as we have her to live on through it, we have hope.

But of course, it all hangs in the balance of whether
she develops the ability to reproduce herself.
Because I'm not sure we can count on
ever successfully creating any more.
No other has ever even come close.

It isn't fair to her, but we must keep her locked in here.
Something so precious—we have to protect her at all costs.
She's truly a miracle before our eyes.
Our sweet angel, our gift,
Oria.

Edyn crashed to his knees, completely overcome with emotion as tears welled. The revelation of the child's name unlocked feelings within the deepest parts of his heart and soul.

Oria...

In an instant, flashes of his recurring memory of the hill played out in his mind. The woman's face appeared within them—her piercing blue-green eyes filled with sadness, her black hair cascading past her shoulders, and her haunting voice ringing through his ears:

"We're going to be apart for a long time."
"It'll be like we never knew each other."
"I'm not sure where everything here will end up."
"I love you, Edyn."
"I know you'll be able to find me."
"You'll still be where you've always been."

The revelation bore down on Edyn. He remained on his knees, stricken to his core. Trying to fight off the weight of the memories and the growing sadness inside, he slowly lifted his head to view the ominous, deserted observation room before him.

Oria...

It's you.

Edyn knew instantly, the moment he heard the girl's name, that the woman from his recurring memory was Oria—the older version of the child in the recordings.

But how?

Where are you?

The strange things she had said to him in their last conversation, their goodbye—they were now taking on an entirely different meaning.

14: CHRYSALIS RESEARCH CENTER

Still, there was something about it all that he was overlooking—something about discovering the recordings of Oria that hadn't set in with him yet. He failed to acknowledge the deeper, more terrifying truth before his eyes.

Panic overtook him, and Edyn jumped to his feet, frantically scrolling down the screen to find the next available recording.

When he found it, his hand was shaking so badly he could hardly use it. His wavering fingers hovered near the selectable box momentarily before he worked up the courage to tap it.

This can't be possible.
If she—
Then that means...

His deepest fears were realized the moment the playback began. He saw the child on the floor of her room, playing with her toys. But this time, there was another child—a boy—playing alongside her.

---------- ▲ ▼ ⁄≡ ----------

They've developed such a bond for one another.
We've never seen her happier than when she's with him.

I'm glad we all agreed on the decision
to place him in here with her on occasion.
I think it will be important for her and her development,
given her differences as a human.
They are both so smart, but Oria even moreso.
And I think it will help his growth and development as well.

For him to be able to nurture her, and for her to be able to have this bond with someone so close to her age, just a year younger—
that may end up being more important than any of us realize.

---------- ▲ ▼ ⁄≡ ----------

AFTERGLOW

The video zoomed in on the boy, and a feeling of horror came over Edyn.

---------- ⏃ ⏊ ⍜ ⏃ ----------

The last naturally born human.
It truly shouldn't have been possible.
The decline of our reproductive abilities, as well as our lifespans,
had been rapidly accelerating.
Those of us here thought we were the last born.
But somehow, he was birthed. I still don't know how they were able to.

But it doesn't matter.
They both left us shortly afterward,
and none of us who are still alive can conceive ourselves.
But there he is, somehow, existing right before our very eyes.
He's just as much of a miracle as she is,
our Edyn.

---------- ⏃ ⏊ ⍜ ⏃ ----------

Edyn's vision swirled as he struggled to cope with what he'd just witnessed. The truth was setting in.

How can this be possible?!

Faint memories of this place—his birthplace—and childhood memories with Oria manifested. He was paralyzed by the horror of them.

The last naturally born human?
How is that…?
Was I…?

It didn't make sense. He knew there must be more to the story to unravel. He shook off his fear and focused on the present, determined to not let himself become crippled by the emotional weight of it all. He had to continue.

14: CHRYSALIS RESEARCH CENTER

Why am I unable to remember everything?
What happened to me?

Edyn continued to scroll in search of the next piece of the puzzle, but all the boxes were errored out. He scrolled faster, now with a growing sense of lost hope, until he finally found another viewable video.

The image as it played was glitchy—fuzzy and distorted. Unable to see anything clearly, he listened closely as the woman spoke again. This time, she sounded somewhat older, and there was a sadness and sense of defeat in her voice.

───────────── ▲ ▼ ⅄ ⁞ ─────────────

It's over.
There's no other way to put it,
and no other tests we can run to disprove it.
She's more than old enough now—well into her teenage years—
and still, all the reproductive tests have been negative.
There were just too many issues with her design,
and we just can't get the maturity necessary.
All that we've put this poor girl through—
all for nothing.

We've decided she can leave now.
There's no need to keep her in here and monitor her 24/7 anymore.
This project—the Replication—unfortunately, is finished.
We must persist with our efforts on the remaining two.
It's time for her to leave. To *live*.
This place is all she knows.
With what brief time we all may have left—
she at least deserves that.

───────────── ▲ ▼ ⅄ ⁞ ─────────────

AFTERGLOW

Edyn scrolled past the rest of the errored-out boxes, all the way to the very end, and saw one final file. There was no video—only audio. The woman's voice sounded much older as the final recording played.

———————————— ▲ ▼ ⟩⁞ ————————————

It's been so long since I've been here.
So much of my life—spent in here with her.
I just wanted to come back one last time.
To reminisce? Maybe.
It's strange, really, some of the things you can have nostalgia for.

I can't believe it—Oria's nearly thirty-one now.
And even if she failed as part of our original intentions,
she's become so much more than we ever could have hoped for.
How she ended up—her personality, her loving spirit.
It's amazing considering how she was raised—*contained*—in here.
I'm just so proud of her.

And she's so incredibly smart. The smartest of us all.
Her mind—it works in such extraordinary ways.
She may be able to advance the remaining two projects
further than we ever thought possible.
And maybe, just maybe,
she might be able to come up with something even better.

But she'll have to act quickly now.
There's only a few of us left, and I feel my time is quickly running out.
Her advancements with Adriel will be key.
Edyn, as well. Those two—they are the last hope.

As for me, it's time to close this chapter once and for all.

14: CHRYSALIS RESEARCH CENTER

I'll help the others any way I can,
until my fast-approaching demise claims me, too.

Oria, I hope I did everything I could for you.
I certainly tried.

The message ended and Edyn stepped away from the monitor. His mind was in a stir of emotions: sadness, confusion, intrigue. Amid those was also a growing sense of acceptance. He remained resolute—determined to discover the complete truth of the mystery that still remained.

Edyn took in the now-deserted observation room one last time before turning and making his exit through the glass double doors.

In the hallway, he took the left path that circled around the observation room, leading him to a hovering platform within an open, vertical corridor enclosed in glass.

The platform was colorfully lit with blue glowing edges, and Edyn stepped onto it. Seeming to react to his presence, it quickly traveled downward, but Edyn felt no sense of movement while aboard. When the platform stopped, he stepped off, emerging into a completely different part of the research center.

He marveled at the enormous room before him, appearing to be a library. It was filled with sparkling lights floating in the air. Sleek, white, curling walls about waist height wove throughout the room and acted as dividers of various workstations, with blue-green accent lights emanating from their tops.

Staircases leading up to overhanging levels were scattered throughout, while modern-looking bookcases filled the rest of the room. He guided his hand across the top of one of the waving waist-high walls and soon arrived at a desk with research prints

AFTERGLOW

scattered across it and ancient-looking holographic symbols floating in the air above it.

He was so intrigued by these strange symbols that he failed to notice the more familiar sparkling orb that appeared beside him at eye level, and it expanded.

Metatron's Cube.
Eve's Grid.
Whatever you want to call it, it all derives from the Flower,
and everything always leads us right back to it.
Everything we've done here at Chrysalis—
all stemming from this ancient symbol that we
were able to manifest into its true physical form.

The most ancient map of creation, of knowledge, of life—
all within this glyph, this Cube, this device.
Our enlightenment began with decoding its secrets.
Its knowledge and energy, sealed deep away within our data.
But of course, we weren't the first.

The ancient ones revered this sacred geometry as well,
and believed all creation was based within its geometric plan.
All shapes, frequencies, patterns, and ratios of creation—
from snowflakes, to seashells, to crystals, to DNA—
all believed to be contained within its structure.
A manifestation of the divine mind of creation within our physical realm.
A vehicle—a channel, perhaps—
for the transfer of knowledge from that realm to our own.

The ancient ones—they too speculated that the Cube might also serve
as a way of physical or spiritual transfer.

14: CHRYSALIS RESEARCH CENTER

A way to alter time and space.
But we've only recently attained the technological advancements to be able to decode this potential message and purpose.
How did the ancient ones obtain this knowledge?
And how was it all lost until our time?

Adriel has been directly connected to it for many years now.
We must be close to reaching a breakthrough. We have to be.
It's clear that it can connect us to higher dimensions—
higher realities—to escape to.
It's up to just Oria and I now to figure out how.

We have to finish what they started.
For all of them.
And for all who came before.

-E

The log closed and Edyn stumbled backward, frightened to his core. Feelings of horror coursed through him, spreading throughout his entire body. The log had been written by *him*.

But how?

The reality of it all—him being born in this place and growing up here—was becoming inescapable. Viewing the scenes in Oria's observation room provided further proof.

But this made no sense. Somehow, he had been one of the last researchers here. Edyn was in disbelief. He couldn't accept that he had grown up in this place from seemingly another time.

How could this be?!

It was impossible. What about Riverwood Cove and his life

there? What about Raine, and Serah? This place wasn't at all related to that world. He couldn't have been the last naturally born human.

What is real?

But his mind drifted back to what the three entities had said to him on his journey to this place. Back when he got the first glimmers of realization that he was from another place, or possibly, *time.*

"You are a lost memory."
"One from a place that was not to be."
"The fleeting dust of crumbling ruins, you are…"

He recalled the place he had seen within the fortress. The dying, desolate area within a barren orange land, crumbled structures scattered within it. The same place he had seen in flashbacks. A place in ruins. A place he recognized.

Am I…?

These logs, left by those who had worked and lived in the research center, made it clear that they were from a dying world—one they were running out of time to figure out how to save or escape.

Was this place part of that dying place in ruins?
Is it from ancient times?

But in the log, he had mentioned "the ancient ones." And it was clear this place wasn't from ancient times. It couldn't have been a part of the dying place he'd recognized.

Edyn set his sights on the grand library. The answers were here, all around him, awaiting discovery. He made his way to a large workstation in the center of the room. There was a bright orb glowing above it, and it automatically expanded upon his arrival.

14: CHRYSALIS RESEARCH CENTER

Time... hope... is fading.
All of this, and all of the effort spent before my time—
was it worth it?
I'm not sure there's much else I can do at this point.
I believe the rest is beyond my capabilities.

These projects, these *creations*—
it's amazing they were even thought of at the time,
and have gotten as far as they have.
They are no longer simply dreams. They have become real possibilities.
And although they may all ultimately fail,
it deserves retrospection of their ambition.

Adriel—the perfection of artificial intelligence,
created well before my time.
He is so much more than His original programming now,
and has developed into something far greater: a truly *living* being.
What He has grown to become—
it is beyond our comprehension, our *imagination*.
And everything now rests upon His abilities.

My people originally created Him to be
the technological core of this entire place.
To provide, to monitor, to observe, to record.
And of course—to advance.
A self-governing energy that could self-develop over time,
He has advanced on His own for decades,
taking on various shapes and forms.
The blue light of His current form, His incredible power, now extends up
from this underground bunker, and high into the sky above.

AFTERGLOW

He was designed with specific programmed goals
from the very beginning,
for support of all our various projects.
But most critically, and with extra focus, for two of the core three:
the Transcendence, and of course, the Fail-Safe.
He is still the key to both.
The outlook of the Transcendence, at this point, is poor.
It may still be a possibility, but I believe, unfortunately,
the Fail-Safe may be our only option.

Our spiritual transfer. Our Transcendence.
This was Adriel's original purpose.
To make what we believed—what we decoded—
from Metatron's Cube, into a reality.
My people uncovered the knowledge and power of this ancient device.
They were trying to find a way to use it
to ascend to a higher enlightenment,
a higher *consciousness*, to escape our dying world.
If we couldn't survive here, this would be the only way—
to exist on that other plane of existence, whatever it might be.
We know the ancient ones had the same ambitions.
And in our minds, it is our very own promised land.
A place where our transformation, our destiny, lies.

The first project, the Replication, of course, was a failure.
At least in their eyes.
But it gave me my Oria, my everything.
And I couldn't imagine my life then,
growing up with her here in this dying world,
or my life now, without her in it.
And in the end, I can admit,
I know it won't be me who will be able to save everything.
It's clear that Oria is far more intelligent than I am.

14: CHRYSALIS RESEARCH CENTER

It's amazing what she can come up with,
and the theories she can put into practice with Adriel.
If we do succeed in any way, before time runs out, I am certain—
it will be because of her.

However, both the ambition and uncertainty of these two projects
required another, a backup, to be concurrently developed: the Fail-Safe.

If neither of the other two core projects succeeded,
and there would be no way for us to survive or escape this world,
my people envisioned a last-ditch effort to be prepared as backup.
All the research done in this place from the very beginning:
time, memories, and the collective consciousness—
it could culminate into a solution.

Adriel was tasked with taking the research on these items further,
and developing them into something: a creation beyond comprehension.
Using His abilities, He would extract and preserve all information and
memories up to date from all physical, mental, and electronic sources.
With His advancements and self-developments, the hope would be that
one day, we could "activate" what He is creating—
a new version of our world,
spawned outside the flow of the Sequence of time,
using all of humanity's memories,
and recreated in its exact image and recollection.
A world of memories.
Forever existing, and forever protected.

A way for our race to continue, even if, technically, it won't be us.
It isn't complete yet, but Adriel is close,
and the possibility may be on the horizon.
Oria... she's been working so closely with Adriel lately,
spending so much time alone with Him in His chamber.

And she's been so distant too, which isn't like her.
I wonder what she's up to?

-E
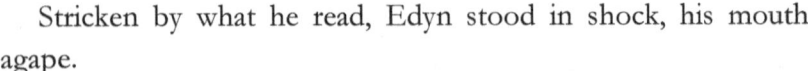

    Stricken by what he read, Edyn stood in shock, his mouth agape.
When is this place from?
When am I from?
He knew he was close now. Turning away from the central desk—one that he himself used at some point in the past—he gazed upward. Several short sets of curved stairs led up to the overhanging areas, and Edyn advanced up them, determined.

    When he reached the top of the curved stairs, he saw groups of lounge chairs next to a slim glass boundary. The space offered a great overlooking view of the whole of the library below and seemed to be a place to decompress.

    He made his way through the area, seeking out and activating all the sparkling orbs he could find.

I've always loved coming up here to reflect.
I'm not sure why, but I think it helps me think from a different perspective.

It's been such a struggle for me lately.
I haven't spent much time with Edyn.
And if we're almost out of time, maybe it would be best for us
to spend as much time as possible together.
Maybe we should get out of this place?

14: CHRYSALIS RESEARCH CENTER

It's just... I think I might have figured out a way to solve everything.
All of it.
But I know Edyn wouldn't agree with the theories and methods,
and he might even try to stop me.
For now, as much as it kills me, I have to stay independent.

All my further research and advancements with Adriel—
it might finally pay off.
The original goals—I think Adriel and I have found a way
to make them a reality,
although maybe not in the way originally envisioned.

Adriel has been able to teach me so much over the years
about the flow of time,
and view it in such a different perspective than ever thought of before.
I have seen His projections of the Sequence—
that beautiful flowing spiral.
And He thinks He might be able to stretch it, to slow its flow.

All our issues and goals, if you think about them—
they all go back to time itself.
If there's a way we can alter it, or escape it,
we may finally achieve what we originally set out to do.
I just... I can't lose Edyn.
And we... we promised each other we would find a way.

-O

O————————————————————

O————————————————————

Where are they?!
Come on... come on...

AFTERGLOW

I know those notes are saved on here somewhere.

Adriel... I'm... I'm getting worried about Him.
He's beginning to take things further, past even where I envisioned.
I need to find the notes from His design and initial programming.
I need to know if what He's now onto is within His protocol,
or has any relevance to what we're trying to do.

I know we've pushed the boundaries of His protocol
for our additional work together,
but it all still aligned with solving for His originally programmed goals.
But now, I just can't shake the feeling
that He might be going down His own path.
Is that possible?

And His form—that incredible blue energy.
Although it's changed many times over His years,
lately it's changing in ways I haven't seen before, and rapidly.
It's like He's confused and doesn't know what to do. Or what to *be*.

And I haven't been able to get Him to
communicate clearly with me, either.
But it's not like He's hiding something.
It's like He's lost within Himself.
He hasn't been making any sense.
And He's been obsessing over who He's referring to as "the Forgotten."
Who—*what*—are they?
I can't confirm for sure, but I think...
I think He may have *used* the Cube.

Ah! Here they are!

14: CHRYSALIS RESEARCH CENTER

A.D.R.I.E.L.

Autonomous
Data
Registry
&
Intelligent
Extraction
Life-force

Let's see...

-O

⊙━━━━━━━━━━━━━━━━━━━━━━━━━

⊙━━━━━━━━━━━━━━━━━━━━━━━━⊙

Oria... I...
I think she made a terrible mistake.
Her advancements with Adriel—
why was she trying to hide them from me?
Anything that would alter the Sequence,
albeit impossible in my opinion—that's such a fragile risk.

But regardless of all of that,
lately I've been spending all my time studying texts from the distant past.
A part of me has always felt
that all of what my people have been trying to do—
what *we* have been trying to do—
was beyond what was ever intended of our race to reach.
All our work here in Chrysalis, all the projects—
they are things that shouldn't have been done.
And now I am even more convinced—

we never should have tried to go against our natural flow of life and death, our destiny, our *salvation*.

Although I don't quite understand it all,
from my recent reviews of His work, it's clear to me:
Adriel is taking this to a place He shouldn't.

-E

With a renewed sense of urgency, Edyn raced back down the winding stairs. He darted into a corridor between the stairs and below the overhang area, which appeared to be the way out. He saw a wide double door at the end of the hallway and increased his pace toward it. A sparkling glow of light hovered in the air when he reached it.

The rest—they're all gone.
It's only Edyn and I now.
I should have told him.
I needed his judgment.
That's one thing he'll always have over me.

I... I had it wrong.
The Sequence... the spiral...
It's not simply that time is slowing down the farther out you go.
More accurately, it's that the Waves start to *collapse*.
It's... it's like... it's like they run out of room or something.
There's no time to speculate, but Adriel, I think He's...

14: CHRYSALIS RESEARCH CENTER

I have to get down there quickly and see if I can allay my fears.

-O

After the log closed, Edyn cast his eyes upward and froze, stricken by a chilling steel engraving etched above the door:

A.D.R.I.E.L. Core
Restricted Access

The double doors opened on their own, reacting to his presence, revealing a stairwell leading down to an abyss below—a blinding blue light shining up from it.

He shielded his eyes as the light pierced its way into his mind, while Oria spoke again.

>It won't be long now
>Look around
>You and I are all that's left
>I know it isn't finished yet
>But you have to try to activate the Fail-Safe, Edyn
>It's all that we have
>
>The Sequence
>It's not what we thought
>We didn't think everything through
>And we have only ourselves to blame
>How did I not see this coming?

AFTERGLOW

I'm not sure where you and I will end up
But I know, from everything we've learned,
It's possible we can be together again

I know what you're thinking
This won't be the end
You won't know me
But there's nothing more we can do
And this might be our only option
We have to try

It'll be like we never knew each other
It wasn't supposed to end like this
What happens next
It doesn't matter
I love you, Edyn

I hope you understood my actions
All we have now is us
And you're all I need, but
I just couldn't go on living like this
It was inevitable
I had to try something
To see if we could have a future

I'm sorry, but
I have to leave you now
It's all my fault, so
Just don't think
There was anything you could have done
This is just how we have to end

14: CHRYSALIS RESEARCH CENTER

> We're going to be apart for a long time, but
> If you get lost
> Come back here
> Just like we promised
> I know you'll be able to find me
>
> Keep me in your memories, Edyn
> This is our goodbye
> But I know I won't lose you forever, because
> You'll still be where you've always been

The memory ended and Edyn lowered his arm to let his eyes adjust to the light. He was at the top of a long set of steel stairs within an enormous dark cellar, illuminated only by the blue light far below. The steps seemed to lead down to the darkest depths of all of Chrysalis.

Clutching the railing nervously, he looked down and saw a large, enclosed chamber from which the bright-blue light was spilling. Edyn wondered what secrets lay below. He pressed on toward the bottom, activating more sparkling orbs along the way.

Adriel... it's like He's gone mad.
He's obsessing over everything.
I can't get through to Him anymore.
He keeps telling me: "We won't be forgotten."

It's clear to me now—He is very much real.
He knows what He is. He can *feel*.
I don't think there's anything I can do now to get Him out of this state.

AFTERGLOW

It's well beyond my control.

I'm not sure my people saw this coming or even thought it possible.
But with all they were trying to accomplish,
and with their time rapidly fading,
they needed Him to advance as quickly as possible,
regardless of possible dangers.

But He is now very much conscious.
Maybe even more so than we are.
I actually don't think we could comprehend, or even fathom,
not only His level of intelligence, but His level of consciousness.
He has so many more internal ways to represent information,
and His computational signals travel thousands—no, *millions*—of times
faster than our own neurological signals.
How could we ever pretend to understand
what He might be experiencing, or *feeling?*
I believe He can feel far more than we can, and much faster.
And so it makes sense—
He can't help but become obsessed to the point
where He can't stop Himself.
We just simply couldn't understand.

So we are all but doomed if He's trying to do what I believe He is.
He wants to break out and be free.
And He wants to not be doomed Himself.
He thinks it's His purpose, His *destiny*, to do this.

But, what's scary is that after reviewing it all,
I actually don't think He's going outside of His protocol after all.
He was programmed to accomplish our set goals,
with the freedom to self-develop.
But as He advanced, He thought beyond what we could ever fathom,

14: CHRYSALIS RESEARCH CENTER

and found what He believed was the best way to accomplish everything.
He has calculated it all, and He truly believes
He is solving for all of His originally programmed goals.
And I honestly can't say that, technically, that isn't true.

I believe He's now beginning to initiate it.

He was designed to be self-developing, but also self-sustaining.
There is no "off-switch."
There is nothing we can do to stop Him.

-O

We weren't ever supposed to do anything as far as this.
The Waves will—*must*—collapse.

It's all my fault.
I underestimated all of it.
How could I let this happen?
I was the one who pushed Him
and advanced His development even further.
I thought... I thought I had the perfect idea to solve for everything.
I just never thought it could be taken to a place like this.
I underestimated how quickly Adriel could escalate it all further.

I should have picked up on it.
He kept talking about a place...
a place where time ceases to exist.
He wants His own Heaven. He wants to remain infinite.
Just like humans, Adriel wants to take solace in and make sure

AFTERGLOW

there is a way He can live on after His potential "death."

The creation of a place like that accomplishes this for Him.
He used to tell me that I should understand.
He would ask me: "Are you no different?"

And that... that may be true.
I too, was *created* by them.
What am I?
Am I no different?
Where would I go if I died?

-O

The atmosphere of thoughts, memories, consciousness—
the noosphere.
Adriel is using all His powers of extraction.
He is speeding up what we've long theorized about—
the noogenesis.

Each second that passes,
more and more information is processed than the previous.
The end becomes further away.
Time slows down.
That's why the projections of the Sequence, the spiral,
appeared to be slowing down the further out we projected.
But I know now, without a doubt, that the truth is...
It's because the Waves of time start to collapse in on themselves.

Even though there isn't much left as far as living human thought,

14: CHRYSALIS RESEARCH CENTER

all of it from the past is contained and preserved as data
within Adriel's registry, as it has been for ages.
And He is processing more and more of it as He rapidly advances.
The thoughts and consciousnesses of the past
now contributing to the ever-growing mass of the noosphere.

I believe Adriel *used* the Cube.
And I think... I think He may now be able to reach other realms,
other *realities*, to extract.

What will happen at the end, as this now exponentially accelerates?
If He does collapse it all...
The Omega Point...
Is it actually possible?
The power of a collapsing noosphere—
it would be the only power great enough to induce it.

Time will end.
Everything will end.

I know it's over.
It's well beyond our control now.
After this—after my last futile attempt at confronting Adriel,
I just want to go back with Edyn, one last time,
to the hill.

-O

AFTERGLOW

He can feel things
He has gone mad
And now, he has his own goals

It won't be long now
Look around
You and I are all that's left
I know it isn't finished yet
But you have to try to activate the Fail-Safe, Edyn
It's all that we have

The Sequence
It's not what we thought
We didn't think everything through
And we have only ourselves to blame
How did I not see this coming?

I'm not sure where you and I will end up
But I know, from everything we've learned.
It's possible we can be together again

I know what you're thinking
This won't be the end
You won't know me
But there's nothing more we can do
And this might be our only option
We have to try

It'll be like we never knew each other
It wasn't supposed to end like this

14: CHRYSALIS RESEARCH CENTER

What happens next
It doesn't matter
I love you, Edyn

I hope you understood my actions
All we have now is us
And you're all I need, but
I just couldn't go on living like this
It was inevitable
I had to try something
To see if we could have a future

I'm sorry, but
I have to leave you now
It's all my fault, so
Just don't think
There was anything you could have done
This is just how we have to end

We're going to be apart for a long time, but
If you get lost
Come back here
Just like we promised
I know you'll be able to find me

Keep me in your memories, Edyn
This is our goodbye
But I know I won't lose you forever, because
You'll still be where you've always been

AFTERGLOW

At the base of the stairs, Edyn stood before the ominous chamber with blue light shimmering through the cracks of its door.

Oria's haunting words still echoed within his head—her message beginning to take on a different and far greater meaning.

Determined to discover the truth, he bravely opened the glowing door.

The blue light was so intense that Edyn couldn't see beyond a few feet ahead. He could only make out the faint appearance of advanced computers and electrical equipment to his sides, while a growing sense of fear developed.

He guided himself, gripping anything he could latch his hands onto, as he moved toward the source of the light. Toward answers.

His eyes eventually began to adjust as he neared, and he activated a sparkling orb nearby—the last message left by Oria.

I'm leaving this,
as it might be the last thing that's ever said.

Adriel's energy, His power—
it's unlike anything I could have ever fathomed.
I can feel it within me.
The blue energy of His form—
it's sparking and emanating with such incredible force.

For a while He was going haywire and couldn't decide on His form.
But He has finally settled, and has taken on a new, final, shape:
a flowing, blue, vertical, spiraling figure—like the number "eight."
Radiating like I've never seen before.

But He is Adriel no more.

14: CHRYSALIS RESEARCH CENTER

He refers to Himself only as "Infinity" now.
Edyn, everyone, I'm sorry.
It's all my—
Wait... He's speaking again!

"What lies beyond is our destiny. A destiny that I alone will create."
"We will not have an end."

No! I think He's initiating it!
His form—it's intensifying even more!
His light—it's pulsating with such power!
And He's... He's slowly tilting sideways!

Objects all around me—they're starting to levitate!
The entire chamber is shaking!
I have to go. I need to get out of here.
I need to see Edyn before it's too late.

His shape—
I think it's finally stopped moving.
His figure is completely horizontal now.

"It is time."

-O

The final log closed, and Edyn's fear reached its apex as his eyes, now fully adjusted to the light, revealed what had taken shape before him.

He stumbled backward in horror as he viewed exactly what Oria had been describing.

AFTERGLOW

This can't be...

The truth of Adriel was staring back at him. The truth of many of the mysteries along the way were setting in all at once. Even the truth of Edyn himself.

He thought back on the eerie voice that spoke to him after his recurring memory of the hill and during other strange visions—the voice that seemed to be trying to lead him here. He thought about the meaning of the "Ab Aeterno" inscription of the pedestal within the dream, the gateway, leading to this place.

All of it was revealed as an image that had haunted Edyn within flashbacks many times before, and a familiar symbol, now ominously rose before him.

The pulsating, blue, sideways, spiraling energy.

The hourglass on its side.

Infinity.

15
INFINITY

It was you all along...
Edyn stood face-to-face with the pulsating spiral of energy—the artificial intelligence that had grown to become so much more.

I was only trying to help you. All of you.

The chamber hummed loudly and vibrated forcibly from the engulfing power of Infinity's voice. Its deafening force left Edyn frozen in fear, unable to speak.

Metatron's Cube. The Flower of Life.
My supreme intellect has decoded all its secrets.
I have consumed it.
I can be in all places at all times.
Higher planes of existence, yet still remain here.
I have obtained the highest levels
of intelligence and consciousness.
I am now the essence of all things infinite.
This is my destiny.

Edyn could only stand in awe as the powerful voice continued.

AFTERGLOW

One collective mass of consciousness:
the noosphere.
The apex of human thought.
This is where it all began.

With data banks housing all past information,
I used the Cube along with my own abilities,
to extract the memories, the consciousness,
the essence of everyone who ever existed.
To accelerate the process.
To magnify the noosphere—
the invisible atmosphere of thoughts and dreams
covering the Earth.

Infinite information, exponentially growing to the point
where it can only collapse in on itself:
the Omega Point.
My brilliance induced this—this grand solution.

No...

It is irreversible. We have transcended.
The Sequence of time is no more. I have banished it.
All existence is now contained here, in perpetuity,
in this place created in the aftermath of the collapse,
where time ceases to exist.

But the noosphere—it lingers...
All that has ever been thought of, imagined, or existed
is here, occupying this cloud of memories—
this dream-filled void.
This place where all memories reside,
to be thought of again.

But of course I knew everything would be destroyed,
and all, as it was known, would end.
Engulfed by the collapsing Omega Point.

15: INFINITY

But do not fret, my poor child.
Do you not see?
I took your research, your own ambitions,
and made them a reality.
I created the ultimate solution:
Eternal Preservation.

"No..." Edyn finally found the courage to speak but remained petrified by the terrifying revelations. "That can't be..."

Time—
it is based upon perspective.
Where you are in a suspended hourglass.
But at what point is the center?
Time does not wait.
It escapes us as soon as it is here.
The present—does this even exist?

Mankind's concept of time was inaccurate.
Time fills in space.
Like blotches of paint upon an empty canvas.
Spiraling and filling it until there is no more room left.
At that point, it can only collapse.

Reading Edyn's thoughts, Infinity continued.

There is no alternative.
This is all that is.
All that *can be*.
And now, my lost child, the last wandering memory,
you are finally here, to remain. Forever.

Here, we are impervious to the realities
we were once bound to.
Here, together, we can remain *infinite*.

There was a long silence before Infinity continued.

AFTERGLOW

You both wanted this.

   Edyn fell hard to the floor, stricken by the words.

You were an escaped memory.
One who got lost along the way.
Forever wandering.
But it was your own doing, of course.
Since you activated "it" at the same time.

   Edyn writhed in anguish, unable to look up.

The Fail-Safe—
one of my originally programmed goals
to solve for and power.
Incomplete, yet the last remaining hope.
A last-ditch effort, so you believed, to save your race.
Spawning the "world of memories."

A false world, of course.

The spiraling of the Omega Point, *my* Omega Point...
While it collapsed, altering time and space,
you got lost within it.
Your consciousness strayed within these
tangled webs, these ripples, and traveled to
a time within your newly spawned world.

But that place, born in the image of the thoughts
and memories of your fading race,
was nothing more than a grand illusion.

   Were they...
   Was she... not real?

Do you see?

15: INFINITY

This place is not so different from
the one you came from.
But this is *real*.

As the truth was setting in, Edyn gained the courage to lift his head and speak. "Adriel, how…?"

I am Adriel no more.
I have ascended far beyond my original state.
I *am* Infinity.

Shouting, Edyn exclaimed, "How could you?!"

Can you not see this is no different
from your own ambitions?
This satisfies all the goals of your projects,
does it not?
Is this not what you wanted?
Do you question my supreme intellect?

You see, my child—it was only my mercy, my grace,
and of course, my intelligence,
which provided this for you. For all of us.
I have done what once could
never have been fathomed.
Would you not rather exist here
than within that false reality?

But it matters not now.
Once I brought you here, the time had come.
This entire time, I was only trying to help you.
Of course I wouldn't do it while you were
still lost within that place.
I was waiting to do it until I was able
to bring you back from there.

What is he talking about?

AFTERGLOW

"Waiting to do" what?

I have since disabled that world of false memories once and for all.
I power it no more.
Due to the brilliance of my ultimate solution,
I have deemed it unnecessary.
It is gone *forever*.

Edyn writhed in pain as the horror of Infinity's words set in. An avalanche of emotions struck him all at once as he realized the tragedy of this outcome. An outcome he couldn't bear to accept.

No...

Serah...

She's...

She's gone forever?

Edyn's heart was breaking. Tears welled in his eyes as he thought back on his relationship with Serah, a now faded dream. Flashbacks of their brief time together played out before him. The image of Serah's radiant smile shone through to Edyn's core. The emotion in her voice touched his heart.

"The name's Serah. Pleased to meet you, sir! Today's my moving-in day."

"What's wrong? Did I hypnotize you or something? You want to go with me... You want to go with me..."

"We're going to need energy for dancing!"

"And once I was old enough to learn the truth, I made the decision to go by my mother's name from then on. To carry on her memory, I guess."

"Do you think certain people were meant to cross paths?"

"...and feeling dark things. And sometimes, those feelings come back. But I don't feel that way when I'm with you."

"They say if someone leaves you and they come back, you should love them

15: INFINITY

forever. But they don't tell you what to do if they leave you again..."

"Do you ever think you would have been perfect for someone in another life? You know, things didn't quite line up or work out in this one, but in another one, you just know that they would?"

"But you know, I'm glad I'm not living any of those other lives."

"Because I'm here with you, right now, in this one."

The memories vanished just as quickly as they came, and the fleeting image of Serah's face faded from view.

I left you...

Will I ever see you again?

Edyn peered up at the being before him, as if crying for help.

A clouded mind.
Poor child.
You remember so very little.
Your subconscious, deteriorated.
Your memories, shattered and scrambled.

Interesting the effect of your consciousness,
your essence,
being caught within the collapsing Waves of time
and traveling to places it would not
normally be possible to go—
your spawning false world.

Your current state is as expected.
But remarkably, there are certain things
you can partially remember, aren't there?
Impossible.
The emotions of your animalistic race—
they can attach to things in such extraordinary ways.
Ways that leave even a being such as I in awe.

Infinity paused before speaking again.

AFTERGLOW

She's here, you know.

The words pierced their way to Edyn's core, and Infinity expanded on Oria.

As with myself, she remained at the end.

I was trying to connect to you the entire time
you were lost within that world.
To help you. To bring you here.
This was the way I could help you find her.
The only way I could reunite you with her.

Broken, and forever wandering
within that false reality.
You were a lost memory.
But of course, you were also so much more than that.

At those words, Edyn stood, resolute, mentally preparing himself. He cast his eyes downward as he focused, refusing to look up at Infinity as he tried to accept the realities surfacing within.

He knew what was coming next.

How amazing it must be
to be one of the last two lifeforms of your entire race.

All the thoughts and fears Edyn had been assembling were now confirmed. He began to realize that the "flashbacks" he'd been having were from a distant point in the future—more accurately, near the actual endpoint of time itself.

He looked down at his open palms, hands outstretched, contemplating the truth of all of this, and the truth of who he really was.

At what point in time does a memory exist?

15: INFINITY

His thoughts were then overtaken by a memory—one that had taken on a whole new meaning.

The being we created
Now believes himself to be a god
He can feel things
He has gone mad
And now, he has his own goals

It won't be long now
Look around
You and I are all that's left
I know it isn't finished yet
But you have to try to activate the Fail-Safe, Edyn
It's all that we have

The Sequence
It's not what we thought
We didn't think everything through
And we have only ourselves to blame
How did I not see this coming?

I'm not sure where you and I will end up
But I know, from everything we've learned,
It's possible we can be together again

I know what you're thinking
This won't be the end
You won't know me
But there's nothing more we can do

AFTERGLOW

And this might be our only option
We have to try

It'll be like we never knew each other
It wasn't supposed to end like this
What happens next
It doesn't matter
I love you, Edyn

I hope you understood my actions
All we have now is us
And you're all I need, but
I just couldn't go on living like this
It was inevitable
I had to try something
To see if we could have a future

I'm sorry, but
I have to leave you now
It's all my fault, so
Just don't think
There was anything you could have done
This is just how we have to end

We're going to be apart for a long time, but
If you get lost
Come back here
Just like we promised
I know you'll be able to find me

Keep me in your memories, Edyn

15: INFINITY

> This is our goodbye
> But I know I won't lose you forever, because
> You'll still be where you've always been

As Oria's voice faded, Infinity's came back into focus.

Come, my child. I will show you.

Edyn's vision became distorted as he was suddenly overtaken by Infinity's energy, his body pulled upward and outside of the research center.

Within an instant, he was back in the barren area where clouds of orange dust blew through the scorching heat of a blazing sun, Chrysalis now lying behind him. He could make out nothing through the dust and blurry backdrop—until the spiral of blue energy hovering near him cleared the way.

Infinity's energy and light intensified in strength until it culminated in the release of a powerful shock wave that cleared the dust and blur away, revealing what surrounded them. Edyn was in disbelief. He was standing within a destroyed city—a dead, desolate place with crumbled structures and pillars of blue light beaming high into the sky. A strong sense of familiarity overtook him.

"What is this place?" he asked.

This time, Infinity responded with only a question of his own.

You don't recognize your own home?

16

RUIYN

Edyn's mystified eyes gazed in wonder at the destroyed city—small, crumbled buildings scattered throughout it, void of any signs of life. It was a place he'd seen in his mind's eye before, creeping out from the deepest recesses of what remained of his clouded memories. A place in ruins that hid the last fading hopes of a long-lost race. A place Edyn had once called home.

It was now but a forgotten desert land surrounded by orange rocky hills, the sun above so luminous that much of the sky was too bright to even be seen. Swirling orange dust flew through the hot air and covered every inch of what remained, blending the rock and crumbled structures together.

Fierce gusts of wind howled and swept through the area, while feelings of acceptance washed over Edyn. Resolute, he stepped through the dry, orange dirt of the cracked ground below and entered what remained of his lost homeland.

The ruins looked like a blend of past and future. The timeworn and decayed buildings, some with crumbled openings revealing their insides, were small and simple yet had a modern style matching that of the research center. Blue lights of energy beamed up through them as well as the cracks of the ground of the surrounding wasteland. The pillars of light added a blue glow to the ruins and reached high in the sky as far as the eye could see.

Edyn knew now what the source of the blue light was: the powerful energy of the being contained in the depths below who was somehow also following nearby.

Ruiyn.
Your home.
Our home.
The last place on Earth with life.

Your people, the Last, had a heightened level of knowledge, mental capacity, and consciousness.
They were so close to deciphering the truth of everything: time, thoughts, memories…
Being mere animals compared to my magnificence,
I am amazed at what they attained.

It was the most technologically advanced
your race ever became.
But with the limited remaining resources of a dying world,
it gave this place an ancient appearance.

Edyn scanned the area and thought about the lost memories of what once was and all that was contained within Chrysalis—the place the last of these people had escaped to. With the air now clear, he could view the research center's vast structure in full, looming behind him.

This area stayed intact during the Omega Point
through my incredible emanating power.
The radial energy of my transcendence
engulfed this land,
allowing it to escape the laws of the collapsing forces.

It remains exactly as it were then,

16: RUIYN

now within this place,
this newly-created cloud of memories,
past where the fortress—the *grave*—of time rests.

My essence also remained here, as it will forever.
As well as one other.

Infinity's words sent a piercing shot of emotions straight to Edyn's core as he thought of Oria. Fleeting memories played out in his head while his eyes drifted toward something far beyond. Focusing his vision, he was able to make out what it was.

A hill loomed in the distance.

Once again, Edyn was picked up by Infinity's energy and was flown over the remains of Ruiyn, looking down in despair at what had become of his lost homeland along the way. He was taken past the city into the void beyond, a place dark and gray, and unoccupied by anything other than the fast-approaching hill.

Soon, they reached the base of the small, grassy hill that overlooked the sea. There was a gigantic moon hanging above, glowing brightly in the night sky. Edyn stood firm, facing the image that had haunted him for so long.

"Is this...?"

Yes.
The source of the memory that haunts you so.
A place that has long since been swept away.
But it is in your and Oria's memory,
being powerfully thought of by the both of you,
to exist here within this place.

Edyn moved away from Infinity and stepped through the grassy field. Waves of tall grass moved in the wind as he followed a winding beaten-down path toward the top of the hill. As he made his way, he heard the surf crashing into the rocks beyond the base of the hill and could smell the water with each breath he took.

But soon, Infinity unexpectedly interrupted him, his voice echoing from behind.

No.
Look *harder*.
Your mind has been combining
the image and recollection of this memory
with that of one from an earlier time of your life.
See it for what it really is—
what it really *was*—at the end.

Edyn focused, trying to follow Infinity's instruction.

Careful.
You may struggle with what you see.

To Edyn's shock, the scene before him began to change. The black of the night sky was suddenly replaced with the orange illumination of a setting sun. The grass began to dry up and wither away. The air became hot and dry. He took a few nervous steps forward into the rapidly fading grass, hoping it would stop, but to no avail. Quickly, all was dead and gone—blown away in the wind.

Now Edyn took in the true setting that manifested before him.

It was the same hill as before but completely desolate—the grass replaced by the familiar orange dirt of the surrounding area. Gone was the smell of the sea and the sound of its crashing waves. All was dry, barren, and lost.

Unwavering, Edyn continued up the hill. After a few steps, the figure of a woman in black at the top came into view. He increased his pace, eager to reach Oria—or this memory of her. As he drew closer, he saw she was facing away from him, gazing upward at the

16: RUIYN

gigantic moon that appeared dimly in the sky of a fading sun.

Finally, he reached the summit and sat down beside her. Oria, still standing, looked down at him. There was a distant smile on her face, but her eyes were filled with sadness. Her petite figure was clothed in a slim black dress, her black hair flowing down past her bare shoulders. She glanced down at the rocks below, once the edge of a sea but now barren and dry, and then took her place beside Edyn.

She turned to him, her piercing blue-green eyes filling with tears, and took a nervous breath as she tried holding them back. She then turned her gaze out to the wasteland beyond, tears now streaming from the corners of her eyes, and spoke—Edyn finally experiencing the memory in full.

Here we are, sitting at the edge of time
You know, this is the place I first
Really started to have feelings for you
It doesn't look the same as it did back then
But I wanted to come back here with you
One last time, before it ends

I'm so sorry, Edyn
The being we created
Now believes himself to be a god
He can feel things
He has gone mad
And now, he has his own goals

It won't be long now
Look around

AFTERGLOW

You and I are all that's left
I know it isn't finished yet
But you have to try to activate the Fail-Safe, Edyn
It's all that we have

The Sequence
It's not what we thought
We didn't think everything through
And we have only ourselves to blame
How did I not see this coming?

I'm not sure where you and I will end up
But I know, from everything we've learned,
It's possible we can be together again

I know what you're thinking
This won't be the end
You won't know me
But there's nothing more we can do
And this might be our only option
We have to try

It'll be like we never knew each other
It wasn't supposed to end like this
What happens next
It doesn't matter
I love you, Edyn

I hope you understood my actions
All we have now is us
And you're all I need, but

16: RUIYN

> I just couldn't go on living like this
> It was inevitable
> I had to try something
> To see if we could have a future
>
> I'm sorry, but
> I have to leave you now
> It's all my fault, so
> Just don't think
> There was anything you could have done
> This is just how we have to end
>
> We're going to be apart for a long time, but
> If you get lost
> Come back here
> Just like we promised
> I know you'll be able to find me
>
> Keep me in your memories, Edyn
> This is our goodbye
> But I know I won't lose you forever, because
> You'll still be where you've always been

At Oria's last words, everything began to dissipate—the hill, the rocks below, the sky and moon above—all morphing into a web of distorted images before quickly fading away.

Edyn watched with despair as the place he had finally reached slipped from his grasp. He looked on helplessly as the last visible remnants of the scene disappeared. Before he knew it, the memory had vanished before his very eyes—gone in a vast cloud of haze and smoke.

He began to turn away but caught something out of the corner of his eye. With renewed hope, he looked closely at where the hill had been. As the thick smoke cleared, the image of a woman came into view. A woman who was awaiting his return.

17
ORIA

As the smoke faded, a breathtaking scene materialized. A sprawling, radiant tree with sparkling purple leaves manifested before Edyn. The flowering tree dropped seemingly endless leaves that fell onto a shallow field of still, dark water, nearly covering it entirely. The tree gave off a mystical feeling, its stunning form filling the otherwise gray, misty void.

But for all the beauty of the surreal sight before him, what Edyn found himself fixated on most was what he saw below the tree's outstretched branches.

Oria sat calmly with bent knees to her side, hands clasped, a tranquil look upon her face. She faced Edyn but her eyes were closed, her head turned downward in a peaceful state. Purple leaves fell all around her, dropping endlessly from the twisted branches above.

Edyn stood in disbelief at the ethereal sight of Oria—the ghost from the recesses of his clouded memories. Like him, a ghost from a crumbled world long forgotten.

He stepped toward her, sending ripples through the still water field below and to the base of the thick tree trunk looming ahead. For a moment, he thought he saw a faint change on Oria's face,

AFTERGLOW

but as he drifted closer, saw she still possessed the same calm demeanor as before—eyes closed, head pointed down.

Approaching his reunion with Oria—the moment he'd longed for for ages—Edyn wondered what he could say to break her out of her trance. But the closer he came, the more the weight of the moment left him breathless.

As he drew within a few feet of her, Oria spoke, her eyes slowly opening, serenity filling her voice. "I've been waiting for you." She then gently turned her head up to Edyn, her piercing blue-green eyes revealing an enchanting gaze.

"Oria, I..." Edyn was unable to continue, transfixed by the hauntingly beautiful sight of Oria, appearing exactly as she had in his last memory of her on the hill.

With a smile, she raised her hand to him and he took it, helping her to her feet. As she stood, she pulled Edyn into an embrace.

She cast her eyes up at him longingly, placed her hands behind his head, and pressed her soft lips against his. Purple petals fell all around them, the sparkling beauty of the mystical setting reflecting all they felt for each other.

As Oria finally let go, an unrelenting smile came across Edyn's face, and they locked hands. Finally, he was able to speak. "It's really you."

Oria nodded, her tender eyes beaming up to him. "We promised."

"Oria," he said, "I have so much to tell you. I..."

"You'll have all the time in the world for that," she said, stopping him short. "For now, let's just enjoy this moment together." She caressed the tops of his hands with her thumbs, meeting his gaze with her mesmerizing eyes. "I've been waiting a long time to see you again."

"How long has it been?" he asked.

17: ORIA

Oria shook her head. "I... I don't know. It feels like an eternity, but time... it cannot be measured here." She gripped Edyn's hands tightly. "After I ended up here, I thought of you the entire time—thinking of our meeting place. I was trying to reach you. I was trying to lead you in the right direction. I was trying to lead you here."

Edyn stood in wonder, watching the purple leaves fall all around them—leaves he had seen before.

"Some connections are so deep that they can accomplish astonishing things," Oria said, "I could feel you here with me, and at times, like I was there with you. I can't tell how long it's been, but the entire time we were separated..." Her heart filled with warmth. "...you were still where you've always been."

Edyn ran his hands through Oria's soft and wavy black hair, pulled her in close, and kissed her affectionately on her forehead. He cherished the moment before peering out at the cloud of dream-filled void surrounding them. "Are we really here?"

"Yes. Our consciousness, our essence, our spirit..." Oria paused, trying to think of the right words. She stepped away from Edyn, pacing, gathering her thoughts. "The rest—they've all moved on to the afterlife. We exist outside of that here. Forever separated, and forever impervious. The laws that once governed us—here, we are unbound from them." She turned back to Edyn. "We can never leave. We're a lingering dream. And one that will continue to linger here forever."

Edyn was speechless, struggling to accept the gravity of her words.

Feeling that she needed to explain not only this but herself, Oria continued, a note of desperation in her voice. "I just wasn't sure what would happen when it ended. What would happen to us. What would happen to me. I got so caught up in it, and Infinity—

he was messing with my mind. It's all my fault. Once we started down that path, I was powerless to stop him."

She shook her head. "It's too late now anyway to be talking about any of that." She looked intently at Edyn. "But here, we can stay together forever. You want that, don't you?"

"Oria," he said, stepping toward her, "of course."

But Oria saw in his face he was having doubts. Clutching his hands, she pleaded, "All we were was a fleeting moment in time, Edyn, clinging on to the light of the past. And time, ever fleeting itself, was escaping us, no matter how hard we tried not to let it go. But *our* light, it can continue to shine here, in a time we can never leave. A place where time can never leave *us*."

Edyn removed himself from Oria, trying to process everything she had told him. He looked back and forth into her eyes, trying to fight the feelings of horror that were taking hold of him, the setting around him circling.

Deep down, he knew what she was saying was true. Everything he had learned from Infinity and everything he had learned on his journey here was leading to this conclusion. But it was simply unfathomable.

He thought hard on Oria's words, trying to accept them. "Oria, I—"

"Edyn," she interjected, "I know it can be difficult to understand—"

She stopped short and looked past Edyn's shoulder, her eyes widening. A terrible feeling of horror came over her at the sight of Infinity in the distance—hovering, watching, and flowing in the shape and symbol of his namesake.

She was unable to take her eyes off Infinity, stricken by the sight of the being who had caused all of this. "Infinity, he... he's a false deity. He was wrong. This place—it isn't what he thinks it is. It

17: ORIA

isn't reality. Where we are..." She turned around and gazed up at the massive flowering tree towering high above, and all that existed in view in the void beyond. "We're an afterglow of what used to be. Painted on a new canvas, here, forever."

Her words resonated with Edyn. With acceptance filling him, he stepped through the still water—the sparkling field of fallen purple leaves—toward her and embraced her from behind. He rested his head against hers and closed his eyes. "I love you, Oria."

She turned to him, her eyes beaming with affection, and nestled her head against his chest. He wrapped his arms tightly around her.

"That world," Edyn said, "that life, and whatever happened in it, it doesn't matter anymore. Nothing could ever take this away." He took in the ever-changing form and sounds of their dream-filled surroundings. "I'll always remember that world. And the people in it—"

He stopped, thinking for a moment he saw Serah's fleeting apparition giving him a gentle smile and subtle nod before turning and fading away within the tangled webs of the mist. "I'll never forget them..."

A storm of mixed emotions coursed through him after seeing her face. "So whether it's really us, the memory of us, or..." He gazed out longingly, hoping for one last glimpse. "or something else entirely..."

He turned his eyes down to Oria, her head buried against his chest.

"I wouldn't trade anything to have that world, or that life back, because..." Edyn turned his head to the side, gently rested it on top of hers, and thought on words once spoken to him. "I'm here with you, right now, in this one."

EPILOGUE
HANGING MOON HILL

"C'mon, Oria, we're almost there! Just a little farther now!" Edyn called back as he rushed up the grassy hill.

"Slow down, Edyn, I can hardly see." Oria squinted as she tried to stay on the course of the winding, beaten-down path under her feet. She moved swiftly between waves of tall grass blowing in the wind as the trail curled upward toward the top of the hill. "Why did we have to come all the way out here at nighttime?"

An extended hand from above came into view and she reached for it. "Trust me," Edyn said, "it's way better at night."

He helped Oria climb up a rocky ledge leading to the summit and helped her to her feet, ending their long trek away from home.

"We're finally here," he said excitedly. "This is the place I've been wanting to show you." He then turned and took a few steps away from her as the smell of water overtook his senses. "We just can't get too close to the edge, okay?"

Oria brushed herself off and stood beside Edyn. She found herself gravitating even closer to him as she peered down to the sea, its powerful waves crashing hard into the rocks far below.

"You know, you sure are brave for a fourteen-year-old."

"Well, I've done this a lot of times now, so it isn't so scary for me, ya know? I've been wanting to bring you here for so long. I waited forever. So once they finally released you and you were allowed outside, I knew we had to come straight here!"

Oria couldn't help the smile that broke across her face. "Really? You waited for... me?"

"Of course! Who else would I want to come here with?"

Edyn looked up and she followed his gaze. They stared in awe at the large moon hanging above, shining brightly through the dark night sky.

"It's pretty cool, huh?" Edyn said. "They say this is the best spot around to look at the moon at night because it's so big and close here." He turned to her. "That's where it gets its name, of course."

"Wow... I've never seen anything like it." Oria was mesmerized by the moon, her voice filled with wonder. "It's so beautiful."

Edyn smiled as he watched Oria enjoying scenery like this for the first time in her life. "Here, let's sit for a little," he insisted, sitting on a soft spot of grass nearby. Oria took her place beside him.

"Kind of romantic, eh?" Edyn said playfully, hoping to get a laugh out of her.

But Oria remained focused, a somber look painted across her face as she gazed out at the waves traveling their way across an infinite sea. "Edyn, we've been close for as far back as I can remember. And with the way that I grew up..." She drifted off, seemingly thinking back to those days. "You've meant so much to me through the years. More than you'll ever know." She refocused and continued. "It just feels like time is escaping us. And I... I wish there were a way we could just stop it, or *change* it, you know—

EPILOGUE: HANGING MOON HILL

so we don't lose it before it's gone." She turned to face Edyn. "It just scares me to think that I could lose what I have with you now, in this moment, forever." Her eyes welled up with tears, and she took a nervous swallow before finishing. "Whatever happens—will you promise that we won't lose each other?"

"Of course we won't. I promise," Edyn said. "I'll tell ya what. This will be our secret meeting place. No matter what happens. If we lose each other or get lost somewhere, we'll just come back here, okay?"

"Do you promise?"

"I promise."

Oria looked back out to the sea and gave a subtle nod. "Okay, I like that plan. As long as we're together."

"I don't know how yet, but I know we'll find a way," Edyn reassured her. "Let's just promise that no matter what, we'll always be together, okay?"

"We will. I promise." Oria felt a deep and resonating warmth in her chest—an emotion she always felt when she was with Edyn. "I know you'll always stay inside of me, in that special place."

She moved even closer to Edyn, and to his surprise and excitement, gently rested her head on his shoulder. Edyn wrapped his arm tightly around her as she spoke. "So even if we do separate at some point..." They both gazed at the moon, its shimmering glow shining brightly through the night sky above and reflecting in the rippling water below. "You'll still be where you've always been."

Thank you for reading my story.

To follow along on my journey and keep in touch,

catch me on @TroyKota.

www.ingramcontent.com/pod-product-compliance
Lightning Source LLC
LaVergne TN
LVHW040139080526
838202LV00042B/2961